MW01148196

CUPID SCORES

RETURN TO CUPID, TEXAS

SYLVIA MCDANIEL

VIRTUAL BOOKSELLER LLC

Dancing naked around Cupid's fountain seemed like a good idea...until the law showed up.

Meghan Scott is not a typical school librarian. When her girl-friends convince her to test the Cupid superstition and dance naked around the statue, she reluctantly agrees. Eager to find her soulmate and start a family Meghan reasons, nothing else has worked.

Former professional football player, Max Vandenburg can't believe his eyes, when he sees Meghan Scott running down the street naked. Seven years ago she broke his heart and did the unthinkable. Rescuing Meghan is the first step in finally learning the truth, but when she refuses to discuss the past, can he charm the real story from her?

When Cupid's arrow is aimed straight at their hearts, can two high school sweethearts learn everything in the past is not what it seems?

Receive a free book when you sign up for my new book alerts!

Copyright

Copyright © 2017 Sylvia McDaniel

Published by Virtual Bookseller, LLC

All Rights Reserved

Cover Art by Melody Simmons

Edited by Tina Winograd

No part of this book may be reproduced, downloaded, transmitted, decompiled, reverse engineered, stored in or introduced to any information storage and retrieval system, in any form, whether electronic or mechanical without the author's written permission. Scanning, uploading or distribution of this book via the Internet or any other means without permission is prohibited.
Please purchase only authorized electronic versions, and do not participate in, or encourage pirated electronic versions.

❀ Created with Vellum

Contemporary Romance
Return to Cupid, Texas
Cupid Stupid
Cupid Scores
Cupid's Dance
Cupid Help Me!
Cupid Cures
Cupid's Heart
Cupid Santa
Cupid Second Chance
Return to Cupid Box Set Books 1-3

Contemporary Romance
My Sister's Boyfriend
The Wanted Bride
The Reluctant Santa
The Relationship Coach
Secrets, Lies, & Online Dating

Bride, Texas Multi-Author Series
The Unlucky Bride

The Langley Legacy
Collin's Challenge

Short Sexy Reads
Racy Reunions Series
Paying For the Past
Her Christmas Lie
Cupid's Revenge
Science/Fiction Paranormal
The Magic Mirror Series
Touch of Decadence

Touch of Deceit

Also By Sylvia McDaniel

Western Historicals
A Hero's Heart
Ace's Bride
Second Chance Cowboy
Ethan

American Brides
Katie: Bride of Virginia

The Burnett Brides Series
The Rancher Takes A Bride
The Outlaw Takes A Bride
The Marshal Takes A Bride
The Christmas Bride
Boxed Set

Lipstick and Lead Series
Desperate
Deadly
Dangerous
Daring
Determined
Deceived

Scandalous Suffragettes of the West
Abigail
Bella
Callie – Coming Soon
Faith
Mistletoe Scandal

Southern Historical Romance
A Scarlet Bride

The Cuvier Women
Wronged
Betrayed
Beguiled
Boxed Set

Want to learn about my new releases before anyone else? Sign up for my New Book Alert and receive a free book.

CHAPTER 1

*C*upid, Texas

Reunions sucked. Meghan Scott downed her second glass of wine. What was the point in glamorizing the past when her memories of the supposed fun years were filled with teenage drama?

Tonight was her adult entertainment, and tomorrow night she had to chaperone seventy-five horny teenagers, with her ex-high school nemesis, Max Vandenberg, where she would try to keep randy students from making the same mistake she made with the high school football superstar.

The memory of what they'd done in high school sent a ripple of need through her. Even now, the memory left her breathless. The best sex of her life and she'd only been eighteen.

"Valentine's Day. Today is the cheating snake's wedding day," Taylor Braxton said, flipping back her blonde hair. "I'd like to propose a toast to his new wife. May she never find him in her bed with someone else, like I found her in mine."

The three women clinked their glasses together. Meghan admitted Taylor experienced her own traumatic life event.

Finding your fiancé having sex with a female officer would be enough to send many people into the cuckoo zone.

"Maybe it was for the best. After all, lawmen are known for being serial cheaters," Meghan said. She tossed her long auburn curls over her shoulder out of her face.

Kelsey, leaned in closer. "Well, if you hadn't found him locked in the arms of another woman, you wouldn't have come back to Cupid."

"True," Taylor agreed.

"I can't believe we're all here together again. Just like the old days when we were young and naive and so vulnerable. Now, we're all grown up and--"

"Still single," Meghan said with a sigh. For years, she'd been trying to find a man who made her heart race, her blood pulse out of control, and her breathing labored, like Max had. No one had even come close. Several times the opportunity to settle had been tempting, but then she thought, hell no. Max wasn't anyone special.

He had been her first, and somewhere out in the world, there must be another man who could make her feel the way Max did. He couldn't be the only one. So far no luck in finding that special man.

"Yep, no eligible man on my radar," Kelsey admitted. "Who would want to date a woman with three pain in the ass brothers watching over her?"

Hell, Meghan didn't even have a radar. There were a few men in college, but none were memorable.

"I don't want a man. I'm giving up. I'm going to remain single the rest of my life," Taylor announced.

Meghan didn't believe her. Taylor had always been the quitter. Things got tough and she bolted.

"Oh yeah, that's the life I want," Meghan replied, sarcasm dripping in her tone. "Always the third wheel when you're around couples. Every holiday your relatives asking if there is something wrong with you or have you tried online dating. Blind dates with your next-door neighbor's son, who is so kind that he still lives with his mother." She shivered. "No, thanks."

"Or your brothers' glancing at every man you bring home like he's a terrorist, and should they learn he's sleeping with their sister, he would wake up six feet under." Kelsey giggled. "They don't know, but I lost my virginity the first semester of college during pledge week."

Now that was Kelsey. Always living on the edge and hiding things from her overbearing family. Secretly, Meghan felt a little jealous of Kelsey. She had the brothers Meghan always wanted that her parents refused to provide. Two nuclear scientists working at a nearby secret lab, Meghan was the result of antibiotics killing her mother's birth control. The outcome: two career-minded, professional *parents* who never planned for children, let alone a precocious child like Meghan.

"Ohh...with someone you cared about?" Taylor asked.

She sighed. "Not really. We were two virgins who wanted to rid ourselves of the stigma. A fumbling, truly awful, awkward experience. After that horrible first time, I concentrated on my studies and not on men."

"What about you, Taylor? When did you lose your virginity?" Meghan asked.

"Prom night," she said, shaking her head. "Billy Ray Smith."

"Oh my gosh, he's married and living one town over."

"Thank God. He was mistake number one. I was young and foolish."

Meghan laughed, thinking of the night she and Max succumbed to the passion building between them. Under the stars after he led their football team to the state championship, they'd celebrated not realizing the consequences of that night would eventually haunt them. "Well, we certainly know who popped my cherry. Max Vandenberg, football superstar jerk."

The three women sighed. Kelsey shifted uneasily in her chair. "We thought we were going to change the world."

Taylor snickered. "I think the world changed us."

Thank goodness Meghan was no longer the wimpy, sappy high school girl. Don't expect her to take second place to anything or anyone. Maybe that was why no man had stuck around for any length of time.

Meghan giggled. "Remember that silly superstition from high school?"

"Which one? There were several," Kelsey said. "I especially liked the one where the football boys had to put a pair of girl's panties on the top of the goal post if they wanted a winning season."

"While the drill team practiced in our uniforms, all our undies were stolen from the girls' gym. I remember going commando, like, yesterday." Taylor chuckled.

Kelsey turned toward her. "Max Vandenberg was the panty thief. Did you hear that he played professional football for the Dallas Cowboys for a while?"

"Until he got hurt. Now he's back." Meghan shook her head, thinking of the muscular, dark haired man whose blue eyes twinkled with mischief. "Right back here under my nose - the big jerk. He's coaching at my school."

Asking her out repeatedly while she tried so valiantly to ignore him. He torpedoed that bridge a long time ago. Hell would freeze over before she went out with him again.

"Why does it seem like many of our classmates left and eventually returned."

"Yes, Ryan Jones is back. My brother told me he's sheriff now," Kelsey said, drinking another glass of vino. "He was my ex. So two exes back in town and another one's married and lives nearby."

"I don't consider Billy Ray an ex."

The linebacker on the football team, Billy Ray had been a

sweet talking con man who held the record for tackles both on and off the field. Romantic tackles that is. Taylor was lucky not to have him as an ex.

"Wonder how many girls fell for that Cupid superstition? Did you guys ever do that one?" Taylor asked.

"Oh no," Meghan said. "I didn't like getting undressed in gym class."

The idea of running around nude in front of a bunch of females never appealed to Meghan. And wearing the regulated gym outfit was a joke. One size does not fit all comfortably.

"Oh no," Kelsey echoed. "If my brothers caught me dancing naked around the statue in the town square, I would have been sealed away in a nunnery until my female parts shriveled. What about you?"

"No," Taylor said, looking at the two women sitting at the table. She poured the last of the second bottle of wine.

She was up to something. Meghan remembered that look and it got her into a lot of trouble.

"You remember when all the cheerleaders did the naked Cupid dance, all hoping to find their true love. How did the magic work out for them?" Kelsey said with a laugh.

Taylor shook her head. "I remember. The football team showed up unexpectedly with cameras in hand and when the squad returned to school they faced suspension."

Meghan had been on the backup squad, and for over a month, they had to cover the events because the girls could not cheer. But in the end, the Cupid dance worked to their advantage.

"Don't feel too badly for them. They're all married. In fact, most of them have babies. If the superstition is true, it worked very well for them. What the hell is wrong with us?" Disgust dripped from Meghan's voice.

Unlike her scientist parents, Meghan longed for her own family. Children, grandparents, brothers and sisters, and big holiday gatherings. As an only child with a few family members, the holidays seemed blah. Meghan wanted the American dream with all the trimmings.

Taylor threw her hands up. "I'm not looking to get married. Right now, my focus is my parents' restaurant. I don't need a man."

Turning in her chair, Meghan looked at Kelsey. "What about you? Do you want to marry?"

Kelsey leaned on her hands. "Yes, I would like to find a man, but my brothers run them off faster than a deer during hunting season. So I'll be working on the boutique I'm preparing to open for business. One year is all I have to make a profit. Or I'll be moving back to the city. What about you, Meghan?"

More than a husband, she wanted a family. The husband was becoming less and less important. The plan was simple. Get her PhD in science, a good job, and then a sperm donor. No need for a man by her side. She tossed back her hair and stared them straight in the eye. "I'm twenty-five years old. I'm ready. My ovaries are beginning to shrivel like a prune. Bring on the right man and I'll race him to the altar."

Taylor shook her head at the two of them, giggling. "Then let's do it."

A frown appeared on Kelsey's face and Meghan felt confused as they stared at Taylor. "What?"

Taylor checked her watch. "It worked for all those other women. Why not us? The superstition says at midnight anyone chanting and dancing naked around the fountain will soon meet their true love. I've never believed in the notion, but hey, I'm game. We've got thirty minutes. Let's go kick some Cupid butt and see if that superstition is real or not."

"You want me to take off my clothes and dance in front of you and everyone else in town, chanting some silly verse?" Meghan said, her voice rising.

That was the most ridiculous thing Meghan ever heard. Sure, frivolous high school girls did this, but grown women with everything to lose went home and slept off the alcohol they'd consumed. But then again, what if it worked?

Her logical brain told her it was nonsense, but she'd done everything right, and so far, she didn't have a man. Not even a steady boyfriend.

"Oh, most people will be asleep and I've seen you *au naturel* before. I'll be too busy dancing to notice you and your jiggling tatas."

Laughing, Kelsey gazed at Taylor. "And you think this is going to work."

"We're late bloomers. Everyone else did this in high school. We never had the courage, but now we're older, some of us desperate. Let's do it."

Kelsey lifted her glass and drained the alcohol. "I'm in. What about you, Meghan?"

In high school, these two girls had pushed her into more illogical and stupid situations. Almost seven years later, the brainless crap was beginning again. But when was the last time she took a chance? When had she had fun?

"Oh, it's starting again. During high school, you girls could get me into more trouble. You're back in town less than twenty-four hours and already you're plotting mischief."

"Oh, come on, it'll be fun," Taylor said, downing the last of her drink and signaling the waitress.

"The temperature outside is colder than a well digger...and we're getting naked," Meghan whined. "Tonight, other women are being wined and dined and we're going to dance without our clothes, in the town square? Something is wrong with this picture."

"Think of the thrill. The tales you can tell your children," Taylor said.

"Daring." Kelsey grabbed her purse. "I haven't done anything like this since college. I'm just drunk enough my logical, rational side is being held hostage by my fun side."

"Are you in?" Taylor asked.

Meghan completely agreed with Kelsey. Her science brain that thought this was the most ridiculous idea was inundated with alcohol while the fun brain said go for it.

With a sigh, Meghan finished her wine. "I don't want to be the only old maid. Of course, I'm in."

❧

TAYLOR WAS GIGGLING HARD when they left the bar, the three of them laughing as they all but dragged Meghan down the street. Why was it the moment they walked out the door, her logical, rational brain had begun to warn her of everything that could go wrong? Everything from kidnapping to rape to arrest.

All in search of the elusive forever love. What was she doing?

"I could be fired if we're caught," Meghan said. "Public nudity is not exactly the proper behavior for the school librarian. My contract says something about a moral issue."

Kelsey handed her the bottle of wine they'd managed to sneak out of the bar. "Take a swig, Meghan, it will give your courage a boost. Besides, we're not going to get caught. We're not stupid teenagers."

Oh, her courage needed more than alcohol. It needed a silencer to take care of that logical voice in her head that kept saying she was a complete idiot for taking this chance.

"No, we're stupid adults," Taylor said, smiling. "Five minutes until midnight. Hurry, girls."

Squealing, they ran the final two blocks to the fountain. They arrived, huffing and puffing, and stopped to stare at the sculptured God of Love.

"Dancing around this statue is going to help us find the man of our dreams?" Kelsey questioned. "Whoever made up this shit is sitting back somewhere laughing at how many fools stripped off their clothes and danced in the moonlight."

"In the middle of freaking winter," Meghan added, thinking her logical mother would scold her and say her emotions had gotten in the way of her logic. And she'd be right.

She giggled at the thought.

Taylor pulled her shoulders back. "Come on, girls, we're doing this. We're going to prove this is either the biggest farce in town, or it's going to work for my friends. Just not for me."

All the doubts returned with a vengeance and her stomach started to flutter.

"I hope this is worth it," Meghan said as she began to remove her clothing. First, she took off the things that showed very little skin. She glanced around to make certain she wasn't the only one stripping.

Her scientific brain calculated her risk of getting caught. The rank was just a calculation, and in order to apply real data, she would need to know how often the sheriff came by. Still, the odds of getting caught were fewer than she'd expected.

"Will it look funny if I leave my boots on?" Kelsey asked.

"Naked. You have to be naked according to the superstition," Taylor said, yanking off her footwear, the cold stones hard against her feet.

"As soon as the church bell strikes midnight, we're going to dance around the statue for one minute. Then I'm putting my clothes on and walking home," Meghan said, shivering in the buff. "You girls are going to be the death of me yet. If I come down sick--"

"We'll have a hot looking guy deliver you a box of Kleenex and chicken soup."

Knowing her luck with men, the chances were it wouldn't be a hot looking guy, but rather a senior citizen.

Kelsey started laughing. "Look, girls, I got a boob job while I was in college. Aren't they nice?"

She held up her tits for all to see and Meghan turned away groaning. "What am I doing?"

"I'm not looking at your breasts," Taylor said, giggling as she removed her bra.

"Hurry, midnight is almost here," Meghan said, her words slurring from the alcohol. Taking a deep breath, she tried to calm her nerves. They were here, they had undressed. Time to get it on. "Let's do this and put our clothes back on before we catch pneumonia."

"We better get some action from this," Kelsey replied, jumping up and down on the sidewalk, nude.

"And not legal action," Taylor said with a giggle.

Meghan folded her jeans and sweater neatly and placed them on a bench. "Okay, I'm ready. Let's do this."

Passing the bottle of wine one more time, laughing and chuckling and hoping the alcohol would give them some much needed warmth, Meghan avoided looking at her friends. She didn't want the image of their beautiful, naked bodies burned on her brain.

"We're being so naughty," Meghan said, giggling drunkenly. If she lived to see the dawn, Cupid could kiss her sweet cheeks. "Never again."

"Oh, come on, next week we're taking you skinny dipping at the lake," Kelsey said.

"Not during the winter, we're not," Taylor replied.

The church bells started to chime. With a scream, they laughed and began to run and dance, giggling hysterically as the three of them ran around the God of love.

Her logical brain was screaming hysterically that she needed a psychiatrist, while her fun side said enjoy this moment, this will never happen again.

"Oh, Cupid statue find us our true love," they chanted as they danced nude around the fountain in the town square, laughing at the absurdness of what they were doing.

"Nuts," Meghan said. "All this is going to do is give us frostbite on our girly bits."

Headlights turned onto the street and they glanced at each other, their eyes wide. Meghan's heart thumped out an African drum beat, pounding a *save yourself* rhythm in her chest. Shrieking, their hands trying to cover their female parts, they ran but their clothes were on the other side of the fountain.

"Oh no," Meghan said panic gripping her.

Red beacons flashed on top of the car. Her logical brain began to scream *run* and she wondered if this is what happened when the caveman saw a lion.

"Run, girls," Taylor yelled. "Run, it's the sheriff. Everyone split up, he can't arrest us all."

Meghan ran like a lion was chasing her and her life depended on how fast she could get away. And in a way, it did. The school board would not understand why she'd been arrested naked.

MEGHAN'S HEART pounded within her chest, her breath coming out like frosted crystals in the night air as her bare feet slapped the pavement. Panic rose inside her and she promised herself a good cry when she reached safety.

She didn't know whether to circle back and get her purse and clothes or keep going. She was freezing as she ran butt naked down Main Street, glancing over her shoulder every few minutes.

"For someone with a Mensa IQ, you're not very smart," she scolded herself out loud.

Amazing how quickly you sobered when faced with life and death consequences. If she didn't have frostbite from this little escapade, it would be a miracle. Her keys, her wallet, everything was in the park.

Her condo was a mile away. She had to keep moving toward her home and hope she could find the hidden spare key.

Headlights turned down the street, and even knowing the

leaves were gone from the shrubs, she dove behind the scraggly bushes, crouching, hiding, praying it wasn't the sheriff.

A red Corvette screamed by and she rose from the bushes. Suddenly, the car slammed on the brakes, squealing the tires, and the back-up lights come on.

Crap, she'd been seen. She started running. Maybe if she just kept going, they would leave her alone.

The car pulled up alongside her and the window came down. She glanced over and her heart sank like the Titanic into the cold sea. Closing her eyes, she groaned. As if her luck couldn't get any worse tonight, Max Vandenberg smiled at her.

"Darlin', it's a little chilly to be out streaking. You okay?"

A tremor tried to work its way down her frozen spine, creating a ripple of heat and awareness.

"I'm perfectly fine," she retorted, continuing to run with her arms crossed over her breasts, her pride refusing to admit she needed help. Part of her wished he would go away. The rational, sane part of her screamed get in his car.

"Out for a midnight Cupid stroll," she said shivering.

He started laughing. "You did the Cupid dance. And if I was a betting man, I'd say the law showed up."

What could she say. The worst night of her life had just taken a turn into complete disaster. If that damn statue thought this was funny, she'd personally knock down the God of Love. She slowed from running to walking. It wasn't like Max hadn't seen her without clothes before.

"Get in the car," he said. "I'll take you home."

"What? Give up my midnight stroll?" She didn't want to crawl into that fancy car with her ex-high school boyfriend.

"Meghan, I know you're not stupid. And if anyone else comes along and sees the school librarian walking down the street naked, I think you'll be looking for a new profession. Get in the damn car."

The sound of a vehicle motor sent her fear soaring and she

knew she had no choice. Jerking open the door of the Corvette, she hopped into the sports car, her heart pounding nearly out of her chest. Close...way too close.

"As much as I hate to cover up all those luscious curves, I think you need my coat. Don't want the cops seeing a naked woman in my car and ruining my reputation."

He handed her his jacket and she gladly slipped it on. The smell of Max wafted around her and memories of the two of them surged through her, but she halted the memory tape before it reached the good parts.

He turned up the heater and she sighed with relief. Though she still hated Max, at this moment, he was a welcome sight. He put the car in drive and they pulled away just as the sheriff passed them going the other direction with Taylor in the backseat.

"Oh no, he caught Taylor," she said watching the car.

"Wow. Public indecency is not a charge you want on your record," he said.

Her chest ached for her friend. How could a night so full of fun turn so bad?

"Where did you leave your clothes?" he asked, watching the cop in his rearview mirror to make certain he continued down the road.

"My purse, my phone, my keys, my clothes, everything is on a bench in the city square," she said, knowing he would tease her about tonight's escapade.

He grinned. "You *were* doing the Cupid dance. Hey, if you're desperate for a boyfriend, I'm available."

Shaking her head, she grimaced, hating being in this position with him. "Been there, done that, and got the T-shirt along with a broken heart."

With a shrug, he smiled. "Second time around could be better than the first."

"Just take me home," she demanded, wondering why he would

consider dating her again. He'd been the one who left for college hating her. And she'd been angry with him as well.

"Do you want me to go back and try to find your stuff?" he asked.

She wanted her things in a bad way, but she feared the sheriff would catch them. As the school librarian, she couldn't be caught.

"I don't think this car can be obscure. And I doubt the sheriff would leave my things in the park. But drive by and see if they're still there. I'll slump down in the seat," she said, thinking she was risking everything after getting away, but willing to gamble it all for the return of her purse.

The car's engine roared in the night as he turned it around in the middle of the street, headed toward the park and that damn superstition that created this mess.

Slowly, he drove through the square and Meghan resisted flipping off the God of Love. She'd let herself be convinced to dance nude around a piece of rock that supposedly would find her true love. Landing in jail was more likely.

Instead, it had cost her dignity. Her reputation was on the line and possibly her job.

"Stupid statue," she muttered, trying to see her clothes as she peered out the window from the floor board. "They're gone."

With a sigh, she shook her head wondering if she needed to cancel her credit cards and phone, and have new locks installed on her condominium.

"What now? Do you have your keys to your condo?"

"If I can find the extra key without my neighbors calling the sheriff," she said.

"Where do you keep it?" he asked. "I'll find it while you wait in the car. Then I'll bring your robe out and you can put that on before you go into the house."

She frowned as she gazed at the man she'd loved passionately in high school. The man she'd given her virginity and heart until a costly mistake. "Why are you being so nice? You hate me."

He shrugged. "I'm a nice guy. I'm rescuing a damsel in distress."

Oh God. Now she would be beholding to him.

Punching the gas, he sped through the streets of town in the direction of her condo.

"How do you know where I live?" she asked.

He flashed that million-dollar smile the cameras loved. The very grin that drew her to him, making her breathing rapid. "Looked you up when I first moved back to Cupid. Wanted to make certain I didn't buy real estate in the same area as you."

"Ha! Like I could afford even a tenth of what you can."

"Probably not."

He being worth millions, she'd been shocked when Max returned to Cupid.

"So tell me the real reason you looked me up."

"Because I wanted to learn where you lived. So when I asked you out to dinner, I'd know where to pick you up. Only you keep saying no. After tonight, I think you owe me a date."

Meghan cursed. Yes, he'd asked her out several times at school, but she'd told him she had plans, she was busy. Anything to keep him from coming back into her life.

Now, everything she feared was happening all because of that damn statue in the square. And she owed him at least one date, but no more. While they were dating, he'd run when she needed him the most and she wasn't going to give him a second chance to show her he couldn't be counted on in a crisis. She was done with Max Vandenberg, football superstar.

CHAPTER 2

*M*ax located the hidden key and put it into the lock on her home. The door swung open, and he walked through the unit and into her bedroom. Weird that he was in her room without her.

Opening the closet door, he searched through her clothes until he found the pink, fluffy bathrobe. Some slippers lay to the side and he picked them up as well. That's when he saw the locket. The locket he'd given her on Valentine's Day over seven years ago hung on a jewelry display.

A burst of longing swept through him as he remembered all the thought that went into purchasing that piece of jewelry for his girl. All these years and she kept the necklace.

His chest ached at the memory of how he saved up money to pick out what he hoped the girl he loved would like. Several months later, the same ache overcame him at graduation when she told him she thought she was pregnant.

At his first mandatory college football camp with the coaches, he'd been terrified he was going to be forced to cancel his scholarship and marry her. And he would have. He would sacrifice everything for her and the baby. But while he was gone, she'd done the most unthinkable thing imaginable. The loss still hurt when he thought of their child. Yet, here he was back again.

It wasn't that he didn't forgive her. Eighteen, scared, on the brink of the most important time in his football career, and the beginning of her college education, faced with a life changing decision. He only wished she had included him. Together they should have made the determination. With the help of their families, they could have raised the baby while attending school. No, it wouldn't have been easy, but it was their child.

Instead, he blamed her choice partially on her parents. Eccentric, odd scientists who looked at life differently than everyone else. And he didn't judge them, but his family was more the normal Ozzie and Harriet variety.

His fingers touched the locket and he squeezed the clasp. It opened showing both of their pictures from high school, his chest aching from the remembered pain. Two innocent faces from a long time ago stared at him. Now they were different people.

With a snap, he closed the necklace, shutting off the mixture of emotions those photos evoked. Determination filled his steps as he walked out the door to the car where she waited.

With a yank, he opened the Corvette's door, and tossed her the housecoat.

"Took you long enough," she said removing his coat and then slipping on the robe, covering her nudity.

"Oh, slippers, thank you."

"It took me a minute to find the robe. Meghan, you could clothe all the homeless," he said.

"Probably, courtesy of a summer job. When you work for a big department store, you get first dibs on the specials," she said, climbing out of the Corvette.

Dang, he kind of hated that all those luscious curves were hidden from view. The years had been good to her and she was more beautiful now than high school.

"Let's go inside out of the cold," she said.

He really should go, but he wanted to spend just another moment with her before he headed home. On his way back from a training session in Dallas, exhausted, he'd been trying to stay awake until seeing Meghan jolted him.

As they entered the house, she flipped on a light switch. "Would you like some coffee or tea?"

"No, I need to be going," he said. "I've done my good deed for the night and my bedtime has come and gone."

Walking behind the counter that separated the living room and the kitchen, she took a cup out of the cabinet and put the kettle on. "Sorry, I still make mine the old-fashioned way."

"It's better for you," he said gazing around her place. Nice and homey. He wondered if her family still lived near.

"Yeah, I'm going to drink some hot chamomile tea and try to sleep."

With a shy glance, she walked to the counter, keeping the bar between them. "Thanks for picking me up. I may not seem grateful, but I do appreciate you helping me tonight."

"No problem. But I do expect that date."

Though he didn't expect much to happen on the date, he just wanted the opportunity to get closure. To find out why she'd aborted their child and dumped him before she'd gone to college.

"Well, it can't be this weekend because tomorrow night we both have the Valentine's dance to chaperone."

With a nod, he said, "It'll be fun."

"If you think keeping hormone driven teenagers from slipping off and having sex somewhere in the school is exciting, your life is seriously boring."

With a grin, he gazed at her. "My life is great. Don't forget you and I were once hormone driven teenagers."

Being a professional football player was the only thing that had gone according to plan in his life. But he was fortunate, lucky in everything but love.

With a shake of her head, she sighed. "We'd be friends if we didn't share a past."

"We are friends with a past that someday we're going to discuss."

He was putting her on notice. He needed to understand why she'd left without even saying goodbye. Who did that if they loved the person?

"No, that part of our lives is over and is not open for discussion. Not today, not on our date. Never."

Anger rose inside him. Her reaction stunned him. Had she just buried the thought of the child they'd created? Did she have no regrets?

"I'll go out with you because I feel like I owe you, but we're not discussing what happened between us. It's over. It's in the past. Let it go. Just don't think we're going to pick up where we left off. We're no longer the same people. I'm over you. You got over me the minute you pulled out of Cupid."

For a moment, he felt like her hand reached out and slapped him. His first year of college had been spent getting over her and what they'd lost. Before he came back from Austin, she rejected him, packed up and left town. In four hours, he went from excitement to utter depression all because she kicked him to the curb.

"Your recollection of our break up and my memory don't quite match."

She held up her hand. "I'm done talking about this. You need to leave."

"We may not talk about this now or even when we go out, but there will come a day. We're going to have a sit down about what went wrong. I insist."

Bristling in her pink robe, her green eyes flashed. "Insist away, but that doesn't mean you're going to get what you want. I'm not the sweet pushover I use to be."

He reached over and clipped her beneath the chin, raising her eyes to his level. "Honey, you were never a pushover. A master of manipulation, you knew how to get what you wanted. Don't ever think of yourself as a sweet, innocent, little girl. I never would have fallen in love with you otherwise."

Not waiting for her reply, he turned and walked out the door. Soon, very soon, they would discuss what happened between them. Questions he deserved answers to. The past was the past, but sometimes you needed to understand why something occurred before you could move on.

THE NEXT MORNING Meghan sat with her friends at Taylor's family restaurant, holding their heads in their hands. This morning she'd awakened confused and embarrassed by the events of last night. The memory of Max picking her up and taking her home like a bad dream.

At school, she'd been certain he didn't like her, and yet, Max did ask her out and not only that, he wanted to discuss the past. What was there to talk about? He sprinted at record speed the moment he thought she might be pregnant.

Thank goodness it was a false alarm, but it had shown her they were never meant to be. Staying together and risking the next time she thought the rabbit died could never happen. So she shunned him, leaving for college early to escape the boy who thought football was more important. For him, it had been a good move.

"What were we thinking? By the way, I have your clothes and purses."

"Thank God," Kelsey said.

"I thought I would spend today on the phone cancelling credit cards. What a relief." Meghan glanced up from staring into her coffee cup. "We're lucky. Last night could have ended so badly. I could have lost my job. And now I'm beholding to the one jerk I never wanted to see again."

Her conscience twinged. Last night had been interesting - like a car accident where no one was injured, but still, the vehicle suffered damage.

Grinning, Kelsey bent over and whispered, "Max picked you up?"

"He saved my naked ass," she said, her voice a growl as her heart beat a little faster. "At first, I refused to climb into his car, but oh no, he insisted. Reminded me, if anyone else found me, I could kiss my career goodbye. What about you? Did you walk naked back to your place?"

The less said, the better about her situation. She didn't like feeling she owed Max a night out, but really had no choice in the matter. One of the consequences of her dancing naked.

Shaking her head, Kelsey glanced at her friends. "My brother's best friend Cody happened to be driving down the road. When his headlights flashed on me, I hid behind a skinny tree that didn't hide much."

The thought of Kelsey hiding behind a narrow tree was comical. Her new boob job, didn't make things easy.

"Oh, dear. If your family finds out, your brothers will lock you up," Taylor responded.

"Cody promised me this would remain our secret, but I don't trust him. Men can't keep secrets," she said. "At any time, my phone will ring and my oldest brother will remind me of my obligations as a member of the Lawrence family."

Laughing, Meghan leaned back in the chair. Though she wished she had brothers, she didn't want Kelsey's. They were definitely challenging. "I can hear your brother reprimanding you so clearly. Does he always keep his nose in the stratosphere? He's a bigger snob than any woman."

"It's that whole family obligation. Keeping the name clear of any kind of scandal or disgrace. The very reason I stayed away from Cupid. The first time I act a little naughty, I get caught."

"Well, at least you made it home safely," Taylor said. "I was afraid to go searching for you and I couldn't call you as I had your cell phones."

"Yes, no thanks to you." Tossing her auburn hair over her shoulder, Meghan glared at Taylor. She couldn't decide if she was really angry with Taylor or herself.

Taylor thought up the asinine idea, but Meghan agreed to the midnight dance, and then to make matters worse, Max rescued her. As much as she hated admitting it, thank God he drove up in the nick of time or there was no telling what she would be facing this morning.

"I'm sorry, Meghan. Until the sheriff arrived, we were having a good time."

"Yes, we were," Meghan said. "I just didn't expect it to end with us streaking down the street. I saw you in the back of his car going down the street. What happened?"

Taylor squirmed in her chair. "The sheriff gave me a break. Your clothes, your purses, everything is in my car. I never want to ride handcuffed in a police car again."

"Oh no. He cuffed you?" Meghan shook her head thinking how frightening that must have been. It was bad enough being naked in Max's car, even with his coat covering the top half. "You had it worse than we did."

"I've never been more frightened in my life. Sitting in the back of a patrol car, naked, handcuffed."

Meghan shuddered, a trickle of fear scurrying down her spine. That could have been all three of them, heading to jail. Her Cupid dancing days were over. "That would be bad."

A career ender for herself, at least as a librarian, and probably even if she wanted a job working for the government. Naked scientist were not their top hires.

"Instead of taking me to jail, he took me home. Since I wasn't driving, he let me go. If I'd been behind the wheel of a car, he would have arrested me."

"Who is the sheriff?" Meghan asked. She turned to Kelsey.

"You said before but I forgot."

"My old boyfriend, Ryan Jones," Kelsey said with a laugh.

"And now he's seen me naked," Taylor said, shaking her head.

Kelsey sighed. "In high school, I went with him for six months. After we got into a public argument in the front yard, my family refused to let me date him. Of course, it was quite a street fight with my brothers right in the middle of it. When the sheriff arrived, my dad convinced him not to arrest anyone. But he told Ryan not to come around anymore. We were done."

"Was that what got you a summer in Europe?" Meghan asked. Kelsey's family had always been stinking rich. Taylor's family good, hard-working folks and Meghan's...the scientist weirdos hanging out in a small town.

Kelsey laughed. "Yes. Later, I heard he went into the military. Never saw him again." She gazed at Taylor. "How's the big jerk doing?"

"Don't know. We didn't talk too much about him, only me. He gave me quite the lecture." Taylor snorted. "Since high school, I've wanted to dance naked around the statue, but been afraid. Maybe there was a reason to fear the Cupid superstition."

"Dancing in your birthday suit in the town square was a little too risqué for me. Until last night when the alcohol subdued my fear," Meghan admitted. But it wouldn't happen again. Even the thought of a second try made her shiver from cold and fear.

"All I needed was a little liquid courage for me to shed my clothes," Kelsey said.

"It was kind of fun until the sheriff arrived," Taylor said with a giggle.

"Now we test the superstition. Who will find love first?" Not that Meghan believed in superstitions or that a Cupid statue could find you love. Give her an equation or a formula or even statistic and she could break it down for you. Superstitions were just old wives' tales that didn't amount to anything but folklore.

Taylor waived her hand and gave a disgusted sound. "I'm not looking for love."

Meghan wanted to spew. Then why had they taken this chance if they didn't want to find love? "Yeah, well you have a funny way of showing you're not searching for a man."

"Hey, I can cross off dancing naked in the town square from my bucket list," Taylor said.

"You're a little young for a bucket list."

Taylor was the flightiest person she knew. Even more than Kelsey. And she knew they all thought she was a stick in the mud since she'd graduated top of her class with honors, but her education was important. More important than being a school librarian. Working on her doctorate, someday she would have her own science lab.

"Never hurts to start early," Taylor retorted.

The bell tinkled above the diner's door and Meghan glanced up. Oh no, here was the sheriff. Maybe it was time to leave. She had a school dance to prepare for.

He strolled up to their table. "Good morning, ladies. Looks like you all survived last night's escapade."

"What are you talking about, Sheriff?" Meghan lied, flashing her blue eyes at him as innocent as she could appear, feeling the need for a defensive move. "The cat and I were cuddled up at home, watching reruns."

"Well, I found your clothes, your purse, and your cell phone on a bench in the park."

Meghan clammed up. How could she respond to that remark, except to admit guilt, and until they tortured her, she would never confess to the humiliating Cupid dance. Especially if he intended to arrest them.

"I don't see any bullet holes in your head. You toughed out the military," Kelsey said, a sarcastic tone to her voice.

"Made sergeant and earned several medals," he replied. "And

you're looking well. Your brothers still looking out for their little princess."

Kelsey stiffened. "Of course."

"Good to know," he said. "Ladies, I will tell you like I told Taylor. You got a pass last night. But if I ever catch any of you strutting around the fountain, naked again, you'll need a lawyer."

"Thanks for that bit of cheery news," Meghan smarted off. Like she would ever consider frolicking around the statue again. Frostbite and a dance with the football superstar were the only things gotten out of their nude dancing.

"Hey, you aren't combing the yellow pages this morning looking for someone to bail you out of jail. The day could be worse."

"I talked them into it," Taylor confessed. "The Cupid statue was my idea."

Lifting her chin defiantly, Kelsey gazed at him. "We're testing the superstition. A scientific study will tell us if Cupid will find us true love. I'll let you know the results."

Meghan wanted to groan. What did Kelsey know about scientific studies? Her degree was in marketing. There wasn't any science in what they'd done last night except maybe how adrenaline pumping through your veins made you forget the cold fewer than five minutes. Then the cold burn began.

"It doesn't," he replied. "Remember before you go streaking again."

"Streaking?" Meghan said, her voice echoing in the room. "That fad died in the seventies with my mother's generation."

Facing Meghan, he smiled. "Would you rather I call what you did last night indecent exposure?"

The table grew quiet and Meghan cringed inside, her stomach aching. That label had never entered her alcohol soaked brain.

He turned to Taylor. "Are you still cooking me dinner tonight? Do you feel like it?"

Reaching up to her temple, she rubbed the spot. "I'm fine. A small headache. But I'll be all right. Be here at seven. I'm going to fix you chicken picante," she said. "It's a new dish I'm trying out."

"So I'm the guinea pig?"

"You'll enjoy the chicken picante. See you later."

A grin spread across his face as he turned and walked out of the restaurant. The door shut behind the lawman and Meghan and Kelsey both turned to Taylor. She was cooking the sheriff dinner?

Turning, she noticed Meghan and Kelsey staring at her. "What?"

"You're fixing him dinner," Kelsey asked, a stunned expression on her face. "The man that broke my heart and left me for the military."

"My naked butt is not looking out between bars. What would you have me do? Write a thank you note? Cooking him supper seemed the least I could do."

Meghan shook her head. Taylor made sense and he had given them their personal items back without carting them to jail. Calling her no-nonsense mother from behind bars was not a conversation she wanted to experience.

Pulling back her straight hair, Kelsey warned, "He's bad news."

"Hey, I'm the only one last night who said out loud, I'm not searching for love. The rest of you are looking for a man."

"You don't owe him anything," Meghan said while Kelsey just raised her brows.

She was one to talk. She promised Max a date after his rescue. That little piece of information she would keep to herself to avoid the lecture on how he'd left her waiting. One dinner together and then they could both move on with a clear conscious.

"After he didn't take me to the pokey, I merely offered to cook for him since he doesn't get many home meals. You guys should appreciate the fact I put my naked butt on the line with the law while the two of you ran off."

There was no need for dramatics and Taylor was a really great actress. "And who suggested we do the Cupid dance? But I will say it was good of you to take one for the team. Make sure it's only dinner. Remember your last love interest."

Flipping her straight dark hair away from her face, Kelsey smiled. "A lawman, a cheater, who is on his honeymoon at this moment, celebrating with his cheating spouse."

Taylor sighed. "You're right. Don't worry. I'm not taking Kelsey's seconds. I'm returning a favor and this will be the end of it."

Kelsey shrugged. "Ryan was my first love and I thought I would die when we ended. He's a risk for women's hearts. He'd break yours as quickly as he shattered mine. Be wary, very wary."

The bell above the door rang and she stood. "The lunch crowd will be coming in soon and I've got work to do. You guys?"

"There is a high school Valentine's dance. I'm one of the chaperones. Ugh," Meghan said, wishing her head would stop pounding before she faced screaming kids and loud music.

Max and her were just two of the chaperones and the thought of seeing him tonight made her chest ache. No doubt, he would remind her of her lack of judgement. And now he'd seen an older version of her body, not the teenage girl who had given him her heart. That girl was high on the shelf somewhere gathering dust. Her eyes had been opened to the power of hurt in relationships.

"Painting is in store for me today. There is still a lot of construction to do before the grand opening. Y'all will be at the opening? Right?"

"Wouldn't miss it. When is it?" Meghan asked.

"Hell if I know. Whenever my brothers are through with the changes I'm making."

Standing, Taylor glanced at her friends. "Ladies, I had a great time last night, even if it didn't end the way we'd envisioned."

Meghan laughed, her head reminding her she'd had too much wine the night before as she softened her tone. "It was fun.

Though tonight, the coach and I are the school chaperones. Yuck."

"I'm waiting for the phone call from my brother where his head explodes in my ear."

Taylor sighed. "Mom and Dad are in South Padre until warm weather reappears or they would have learned about our shenanigan. At twenty-five, I can hear the lecture now."

Walking out the door, Meghan glanced toward the square in town. The memory of the chill, her cold feet as she ran around the God of Love. Max driving past her and then backing up and telling her to get in the car.

Today, he was more handsome than the gangly boy of seventeen. Today, his arms and chest rippled with muscles the boy had yet to achieve. But his smile, his sense of humor, and the way he gazed at her were all the same. And damn, but her heart still speeded up at the sight of him. Just one of Max's grins spread happiness all through her.

She had to remember, in one of her darkest moments, when she'd been frightened out of her mind, Max deserted her.

MAX STOOD next to the refreshments. Canned soda - no punch bowls allowed due to the many attempts at spiking the lemonade. Now sodas and fresh cookies were the snacks of choice at the dance.

Parents tasked with the responsibility of keeping the cookie trays loaded and the drinks flowing sometimes strayed. Some folks were too busy watching their kids and embarrassing their daughter or son with their date, standing around in groups, pointing to their children.

Meghan stood talking to several teachers, glancing at him shyly. Waking up this morning, she must have been a little embarrassed. Being picked up naked by an ex-boyfriend must be unnerving. The memory of her sweet womanly body was never far away.

The music changed to a hauntingly familiar tune. He stared across the room at her, all the memories flooding him. That song was their song. The one they turned up every time they heard it in the car. The one they slow danced to at the prom. The one playing in his car the first time they made love.

Unable to stop his feet, they started moving toward her. Surprisingly, she met him halfway and automatically, they fell into step.

"You remembered," he said, his voice husky.

"Of course. I haven't forgotten anything about our time together."

An impulse to say something that would spoil the mood sat on the tip of his tongue, but instead he kept the smart comment to himself. Why couldn't he let go of the past. Why couldn't he let go of her?

The urge to pull her in close was tough to ignore, but they didn't need speculation about the two of them running rampant at school. Especially considering some of the old administration was still here and they remembered the M&M romance. Even since his return, the teachers who had been around teased him about what they'd been called in high school.

"Did you recover from last night?" he asked, thinking he should say something to squelch all the feelings gathering like a storm inside him.

"Yes," she whispered her voice sounding odd. "Most of the day I had a headache. Lots of fluids later, I'm better."

"Good. Did you find your purse and clothes?"

A sarcastic laugh escaped from between her lips. "Oh yeah, Taylor had them. The sheriff let her go with a warning for all of us and even took her home."

Max nodded. "Ryan Jones is a good man."

They danced a few more moments together, the silence

awkward and yet familiar. This ballad had been theirs and while in college, he destroyed the CD. Not wanting to hear the one melody that reminded him of her and brought back so many painful memories.

"I watched you get hurt on television," she blurted out surprising him. "I worried about you."

Warmth spread through him. "Yeah, it wasn't good. Torn ACL. The final blow to a career I loved."

She gazed into his eyes, her emerald eyes sympathetic. "Why didn't you go into broadcasting or training with a big team."

After the injury, deciding his next steps had been difficult, and quickly he came to the realization, he lived to be involved in the game.

"The only team with an opening for a trainer was up in Buffalo. I'm a Texas boy and I didn't want to just be a trainer. I want to coach and train high school boys. I want to help them receive a scholarship if they work hard enough. Working in twenty below weather didn't appeal."

"So you came back here," she said, gazing into his eyes.

"Why did you come back?"

"Ran out of scholarship money. With my four-year degree, I decided to work while I'm getting my masters. Then I'll go for my PhD. Cupid needed a school librarian and I wanted to come home. So, here I am."

The song ended and reluctantly he released her, missing the feel of her in his arms, the jasmine scent of her perfume. Standing in the middle of the gym, they stared at one another, memories flooding his senses before they hurried off the dance floor.

"I've got to check the locker rooms. The doors are locked, but sometimes the kids find a way to crawl through a window," Meghan said licking her lips.

"I'll go with you. It's better if there are two of us for safety reasons," he said, knowing it was an excuse to spend more time with her.

Leaving the gymnasium, they walked along the hall to the girls' locker rooms. Pulling a set of keys from her pocket, she opened the door and flipped on the lights. There was no one there, but together they looked in every shower, every office to make certain kids weren't hiding.

"All clear," she called. "Now let's go check the boys."

The music blared from the gym as they strolled to the boys' side. "What are you getting your masters in?"

"Nuclear physics. Eventually I hope to go to work where my parents are," she said. "The pay is triple what I'm making as the Cupid librarian. Plus, I think I'll enjoy working at the lab."

When they reached the other side of the building, she pulled out her keys, pushed open the door and turned on the light. A young couple in the midst of a kiss that screamed trouble jumped apart, staring at them in surprise.

"Jordan and Blaine, you know you're not supposed to be in here," Max responded in his teacher's voice. These kids were the M&M couple of their day. He hoped their ending was happier than his and Meghan's.

"The door was open and we walked in," the boy said, taking his girlfriend by the hand.

"No making out on school property," Meghan advised. "Leave the area and don't come back. We'll let this time go, but if I catch you again tonight, detention."

"Thanks, Coach, Miss Scott," Jordan said and the two hurried out the door.

"Didn't we get caught as kids?"

A frown marred her forehead.

"If I recall, I had you up against the wall," he pushed her against the wall in the boys' locker room just like years before. "My hand was caressing your head, but in my mind, it was your breast."

Giggling like she was eighteen again, she smiled. "Your tongue was down my throat when Mrs. Blankenship walked through those doors."

"Let's try again," he responded, his mouth inches from hers, his brain filled with the sweet, intoxicating scent of Meghan. His lips crushed hers and he felt like he'd come home. Truly home for the first time in years. The sweetness of Meghan surrounded him as he plundered her mouth.

She gave in to the kiss, letting him explore her mouth, her arms slipping around his neck, leaning into him. Her luscious breast - those beautiful orbs smashed against his chest, her center snug against him, her lips subtly returning his kiss. She could protest, but her body said something totally different.

His hands reached to find the nipples he glimpsed last night when she pulled away. Gasping for breath, her reaction slow as she raised her fingertips to her lips. He could see the questions forming in that damn sexy brain of hers.

Just then the door slammed open and two of the kids on his team came laughing and pushing through the entrance.

"Back right out the way you came in," he told them. "This area is off limits."

"You're in here," a kid mouthed off.

"Smart kid," he said. "We're making the rounds. Now if you want to stay that's fine, but that will be five miles on the track come Monday morning."

"No, sir," the two boys said as they scrambled out the door.

As he turned around, Meghan's eyes were locked on him.

"We better go back out there."

"Okay," he responded, trying to act like the kiss meant nothing. During his football days, he kissed a lot of women and slept with even more interested in only his bank account. Yet Meghan's ragged breath, dilated eyes, screamed that the spark between them as kids glowed much like an ember waiting to be ignited.

The dance, the kiss had done nothing but bring back the desire connecting them until it all fell apart.

"Look, I know I agreed to a date, but we're not doing this again. Tonight, that song..."

"Brought up all the old memories and feelings," he finished for her, wanting her to know he felt it too. "We're going out next Saturday. Be sure to pack an overnight bag as we'll be staying in Dallas."

"No," she said, her eyes widening. "I can't. I won't stay the night with you."

He held up his hand, knowing in advance her response. The arrangements were already made to what he hoped would please her.

"My assistant reserved two separate rooms," he assured her. "The basketball game ends late. I'm not taking a chance of driving us home after midnight with the drunks."

Too many near misses driving home at night from Dallas to Cupid convinced him to stay in a hotel. Sure, it was only three hours away, but they would be tired and it would be easier to spend the night. While nothing would make him happier than to share a room with her, that wouldn't happen on this date.

"All right," she said. "But we're looking forward not backward."

With a laugh that was partly hurt and partly surprise, he watched her fidget. "You really are hung up on discussing our past."

"Your memory has gotten the facts a little twisted. The way I remember that summer is being crushed when you left town."

Turning, she walked out the door. Why did he get the feeling he was missing a vital piece of information? What the hell was she talking about? Soon, he would insist they discuss the past.

CHAPTER 3

*M*eghan sat next to Max in the arena. The drive here in his flashy red Corvette had been filled with moments of tension. Once he tried to bring up the past and she'd given him a glance that clearly said don't go there. Quickly, he backed off. She didn't want to start a "he said, she said" scenario with each of them accusing the other.

In her mind, it was clear. Her pregnancy scare had frightened him into running to Austin to be with his football buddies while she anxiously waited for the doctor to confirm the pregnancy test.

In the end, they dodged a huge bullet. For some reason, the pee stick tested false positive, which the doctor told her happened on occasion. But he should have been there by her side. Holding her hand, soothing her and helping her decide what they were going to do.

Thank goodness, the whole event had been an eye-opening experience that showed when things got rough, he ran to football.

"Look, he said, "there's Stephen Rose. He has more turnovers than anyone in the league," he said leaning in close to her.

"Yeah, but Paul Durant has almost as many," she replied.

Max turned to gaze at her like he couldn't believe what he was seeing. "I knew you like basketball."

A smile crossed her face, she loved surprising people with facts. They looked at her and thought *dumb redhead* and then she would drop a few facts that let them know she wasn't all fluff. Max knew she wasn't dumb, but still it was fun to shock him. It kept the playing field equal.

"Football is better. But I enjoy watching the people at the event and I love doing the math. In my stats class, we did research to determine which teams have the best players in the NBA. We presented our statistics to the teacher to prove why we thought our team would win. With that assignment, I got to know the players intimately," she said smiling. "Not physical intimacy, statistics intimacy."

The statistics class had challenged and excited her. She enjoyed putting the numbers together to see what information they would share.

His forehead drew together in a frown. "That's a great project for my players. They could do that with the team they're playing each week. It would help them understand which player to tackle. Excellent idea."

"You're welcome."

"You surprised me the other night when you said you saw me get hurt," he said low.

She glanced at him. "I like football. I've watched it my entire life and when you played for Dallas, I caught the game every week. I also saw you play for Texas."

Watching the run that injured him, had been tough. Sure, she was over him, but to see someone you once loved get hit so hard and not walk off the field, your heart ached. All his life he said he would play professional ball, and then only to last two years must've been be heartbreaking. Maybe it was a blessing.

"Football has always been an important part of your life," she said, remembering the dreams of a high school star. "So I wasn't surprised to see you were a coach. I am shocked you came back to Cupid."

"It's only until I take the boys to state and then I'll be going to a college team," he said picking up her hand.

The feel of his large hand covering hers had her looking up into his blue eyes. A warmth trickled down her spine, awakening all those old feelings. Quickly, she put a stop to the emotions and reminded herself this was an obligatory date to repay him for his help. Nothing more.

"You'd leave behind our small town?"

"Cupid is home, but to coach college or professional ball, I'll move. What about you? If you become a big-time scientist, what if you're not hired at the lab where your parents work? Are you going to move out of Cupid?"

The idea of leaving Cupid was sad, but to do what she loved, working for a government agency, sounded phenomenal. "Yes, I'll leave."

The mischievous grin on his face was one she remembered so well. "We should leave together."

"Uh, no," she responded, removing her hand and gazing out at players. The second half was about to start when the music started. Glancing up, she stared at the kiss cam zooming in on couples in the audience. Three rows behind the bench, they appeared on the screen.

"Meghan, we're on the kiss cam," he said and before she could stop him, he pulled her to him and laid his mouth across her lips.

For a moment, she felt stunned while the crowd cheered. Heat spread through her. This was Max. The man, the boy, who with just a touch could make her body respond. After all these years, he still had the ability to make her tingle.

Finally, he released her mouth. "I think they're gone," he said breathlessly.

Stunned, she raised her fingers and touched her mouth, shaking her head at him. "No. No. No. No..."

"What?" he asked with a laugh. "It was the kiss cam. We're just having fun."

The memory of the months after his dash to college in Austin while she attended Texas A&M made her recoil. Hurt, disillusioned, and determined not to give him a second chance, she focused on her schooling. Now, here they were seven years later, and once again, he reawakened her senses. Filled her mind with things long forgotten.

"Watch the game. Russell Johnson is up and he's the player with the most points in the league."

A grin spread across his face as he shook his head in amazement. "Do you know how much I enjoy being with you? You always surprise me."

A man sitting four seats from them pitched forward. "Hey, aren't you Max Vandenberg? Didn't you use to play for the Dallas Cowboys?"

Max frowned. "Oh no." He leaned back and spoke to the man. "We'll talk later."

"A fan?"

"Occasionally, I still get recognized."

As soon as the final buzzer sounded, he hurried her onto the court and away from the gathering crowd of fans who recognized him. "Let's go. I'd like to have a quiet dinner. Someplace we can talk."

EVEN BEING semi-famous sometimes had its downfalls. Sure, he enjoyed being a professional football player, but the public thought you belonged to them and when they wanted an autograph, you were to produce. Since he'd been released it was better, but still occasionally, he ran into that fan who you wanted to run from.

Plus, he feared getting caught in a situation with Meghan. If a bunch of people mobbed him, she would never would go out with him again.

They reached the Corvette and he helped her inside and then went to his side. As he started up the car, he glanced at her. Like a beacon, her soft auburn curls drew him, making him want to tangle his hands in her hair and kiss her senseless.

"It's late. How hungry are you? Do you want fancy or would you prefer pancakes and eggs?"

She grinned. "You sly devil. You remember I love breakfast at midnight. Pancakes."

"Trying to make the lady happy."

There was a breakfast restaurant not far from their hotel. In a matter of minutes, they sat across from one another sipping coffee. Checking out the assorted patrons at the diner, his worst suspicions were confirmed. Some of these people had been bar hopping and stopped to sober up.

"That was a fun game," she said. "I really thought they were going to lose it toward the end. The seats were perfect, listening to the coaches talking to the players. Oh, I learned so much about how those stats are applied to the game."

There was something so sexy about a woman who enjoyed sports. Even in high school, they shared the love of competition. Only Meghan competed by challenging herself in her studies, graduating as valedictorian.

"You're smart enough, why aren't you going to medical school?" he asked, curious, knowing she'd considered it.

"I quickly learned I don't do well at the sight of blood. I'm okay when it's just a little bit, but a gaping wound in the human body makes me pass out. No, I'm not proud of the fact."

As he picked up his coffee, he smiled. "I don't remember you being a wimp who passed out easily."

"I'm not. Something about the smell, the gushing of blood, the organs, caused me to keel over. Second year in biology and they're calling an ambulance because I'm in a dead faint. The professor told me that maybe I should consider another major."

"Why nuclear science," he said. "You never wanted to be like your parents."

Nodding, she met his gaze. "True, I didn't. But they have great government jobs. And I do find atoms fascinating. I'm considering becoming a professor. Whatever I do, I have to become Dr. Meghan Scott first."

Meghan was the smartest person he knew. Certainly, he wasn't stupid by any means, but she was brilliant. So much so that in high school, he often wondered what she saw in him.

"When I first met you, I was attracted to your beauty, but then I got to know you, and frankly, I like your mind even more. You're smart and witty and to a seventeen-year-old boy, you were a sweet wet dream."

"Gross," she said laughing at him. "Here, I thought you were going to give me a compliment and then you yucked it up."

She acted grossed out, but he could also see she was smiling. The best thing he remembered about their time together was the laughter. The fun.

"Can't be too serious. It is after all, our first date."

"Well, you don't talk about that kind of stuff on a first date," she scolded. "No wonder you're still single."

"Why haven't you gotten married and settled down with a half dozen kids," he asked, thinking how any man could resist her.

With a shrug, she sighed and picked at her straw wrapper. "Seems like I go out with gene pool rejects. A couple of times there was a serious boyfriend, but no one that made me want to wear white lace." Her eyes narrowed at him. "What about you? Why didn't some society girl yank you up in college? After all, a professional player, big money, fancy cars, loose women."

For years, he wanted to settle down, but every time he

thought he'd found someone, he compared them to Meghan and not many women could outshine her. And then there was his ambition. Until he was drafted, women were not a priority. When he played professional ball, he was leery of the football bunnies.

He laughed. "Several tried to convince me, but no one I wanted to meet in front of a preacher. Lots of football bunnies, but I didn't want to spend forever with a girl looking for a sugar daddy and her next plastic surgeon." Glancing at her with a grin, he winked. "I guess I've always been drawn more to brains than beauty."

Sitting across from Meghan, an excitement he hadn't felt in years filled him. Why was he drawn to this woman? Why did she make him forget the world around him and make him dream of once again taking her? His chest ached with the need to touch her and he reached out and grabbed her hand.

"You are so smooth," she tsked just as their food arrived, removing her palm from his. "Too bad I don't believe you. But you get an A for being creative. Men don't want to marry a woman with brains. They want someone who looks like a beauty queen in public and acts like a porn star in bed." Picking up her fork she pointed it at him. "And jocks are the worst."

EARLY THE NEXT MORNING, Max went down to the hotel's workout room. Last night when they checked into the hotel, she disappeared into her room before he could kiss her goodnight.

Once the bellman took their luggage upstairs, set it down and walked out of the room, while Max tipped him, she shut the door. Leaving him sheepishly gazing at the closed portal.

Never before had a woman rejected him so completely. It was obvious, she wouldn't sleep with him, but still he wasn't afraid to try. And a kiss goodnight...he thought that was in the bag.

With a right hook, he slammed the weight bag and wondered when he should ask her about the baby. So far they were having a good time and he didn't want to ruin his reconciliation efforts. At this moment, he didn't know what he wanted with Meghan.

She requested they leave before noon as she had homework to complete.

Right now, he was planning for the spring workouts and there would be tryouts soon for varsity. Sorry, but on his team, you weren't automatically promoted. A hard-working player earned a spot to play football.

Running on the treadmill, he looked up in time to see Meghan, in a two-piece bikini clinging to her curves, her red curls in a clip, dive into the water. That bathing suit would not be allowed out of the house if she was his girlfriend. Those luscious curves would be for his eyes only and yet he couldn't say anything.

His workout ended a little early as he couldn't concentrate knowing she was swimming on the other side of the glass wall. He left the gym and walked over to join Meghan.

With a splash, he dove in and came up beside her shaking the water out of his eyes. Right next to him, she floated, watching him, her large green eyes staring at him. "Good morning."

"Morning," she said. "Did you sleep well?"

"Would have been better if you'd been by my side," he said.

"Man, you must never get any rest. You're such a deprived man," she teased.

"One minute the bellman was putting your luggage in the room and the next I was standing out in the hall, all alone."

"Poor baby," she said and started to swim away.

Stroke for stroke, they swam the length of the pool, side by side.

Finally, she stopped, breathing hard, her hand resting on the concrete wall. "I haven't been swimming in forever. I couldn't resist."

"Come over to the house this summer. We'll go swimming," he said.

She threw up her arm. "Of course, you have a pool."

He grinned. "You have one at your condo complex."

"Yeah, I do, but it's winter and usually I avoid the concrete pond in the cold."

One of the first things he bought when he got the first professional contract was a house with a pool. As a kid, he wanted one, and now his hard work had paid off and he purchased that dream. He swam up next to her trying not to notice the curves her swimsuit showcased. "Where did you get the bikini. Nice."

"Summer job," she said. "The job had lots of excellent perks, but I don't miss the work."

Feeling the need for the kiss he missed out on last night, he placed his arms on either side of her, trapping her. She stared at him, her emerald eyes wide. "What are you doing?"

"What I've wanted to do since the night of the Valentine dance. I'm going to kiss you," he said and his mouth covered hers.

They were the only ones in the pool area. Soaking wet, he pulled her against him, giving her mouth a thorough tasting, slanting his lips over hers. There was still so much passion between them. So much they could explore if only she gave them a second chance.

Did he want another chance with Meghan? Since his return to Cupid, he told himself he needed to talk to her, find out how she made the decision about their baby. He had to understand how she gave up the life they created. He had to know why she wouldn't discuss the alternatives with him first.

Instead, they danced around each other and now they were in the water and all he could think about was removing her skimpy outfit. About her breasts smashed against his chest, his dick hardening in the vortex of her thighs.

Like a big stop sign, she pushed her hand against his chest, breaking the seal of their lips. At first, she simply stared at him, shaking her head.

"Don't tell me you didn't enjoy that," he said. "Twice now we've shared an intimate kiss and both times you've responded."

Her breathing heavy, her eyes dilated. "Just because I respond to your kiss doesn't mean I'm ready to jump back into the fire with you. I've been burned once. Why would I want to risk getting hurt again?"

His breathing labored, he wiped the water from his face and stared at the beautiful woman in front of him. Longing filled him and he wanted to take her right here, right now. But there were things between them that needed resolving.

"I don't understand why you think you're the injured party. Tell me how I hurt you."

The most important football camp of his life and when he returned, she'd been gone. No notice, she left.

"You don't think ..." she stopped, her body tensing, her eyes widening and he remembered that look. That was an oh shit, I'm so mad, you're going to regret living glare. "No," she said sharply, her voice echoing in the enclosed room. "I am not talking about the past with you. It's over. It's done."

"Don't you think it would help us both understand if we talked about what we did wrong?"

Splashing through the water, she walked to the edge of the pool. "I'm going upstairs, packing my bags and calling one my friends to come pick me up. We're not doing this."

"All right. I'll take you home. I promise I won't bring it up again."

"I mean it, Max. I'm not discussing this with you again."

CHAPTER 4

*D*amn it to hell. Sitting in the school parking lot, she turned the key again, knowing she had an online class tonight, needing to get home.

Possibly, the last cold front of the season had rolled in, gusting the north wind to over thirty miles an hour while the temperature plummeted. One thing about Texas, the weather never stayed the same long. Yesterday, seventy-five, and today, forty with ice predicted later tonight.

And now, her car wouldn't start.

The sun sat low in the west, more hazy than sunny with clouds chasing the sunshine away. Getting out of the car, she lifted the hood and checked the connection on her battery. All she knew to do was try tightening the cables, praying that solved the problem.

Climbing back in the car, she turned the key and heard the distinctive sound of click, click, click. The urge to pound her hands on the steering wheel was strong, but she leaned her head back, closed her eyes and sighed. Just what she didn't need.

A knock on the window had her jumping, her eyes turning to see who was there.

"What's wrong?"

Max. Since their date, he had become her shadow, showing up in the teacher's lounge at her every break.

"It won't start," she said with a sigh as she picked up her cell phone. "Let me call the car service."

"Hang on, if the problem is the battery, I can start the car," he said, jogging several cars over to the Corvette. He probably carried jumper cables, but how would they reach to her car. Other automobiles were parked between them and she was blocked in.

He came back carrying a small box with jumper cables attached.

Huddled in the car, she stepped out, wrapping her coat around her tightly. "What's that."

"It's a jump starter," he said. "If it works correctly, I should be able to start your car."

"That little thing?"

Connecting the cables, he turned to her. "Turn the key."

Glad to get out of the cold biting wind, she crawled into the vehicle and turned the key. In amazement, the engine started. Relief flowed through her and she let the motor idle for several moments before she left the warmth.

With a slam, he closed the hood of the car and faced her. "All fixed, for now."

"Thank you," she said and impulsively gave him a hug. "This means I don't have to sit and wait."

"No, but you should take the car to a mechanic and buy a new battery. The cold has done yours in. I'll follow you to Fred's garage. He's a friend. He'll change it out right away."

A sense of relief filled her. Her car was not the best, but while attending school, she didn't have the money to purchase a newer model. "You've already helped me so much, you don't have to accompany me."

"Look, I want to go home and relax; not worry, you're

stranded in this jalopy along the road. Besides, I'm headed that direction," he said.

"Thanks, Max," she said, feeling a little unnerved. Had the years since high school changed him. In the past, he'd never been this protective or helpful. But then again, he'd been a young football star, his interest focused on playing college ball.

"See you tomorrow," she said and crawled behind the wheel.

The next day, when she arrived in the library, a gift bag sat on her desk and wondered which student was buttering her up because he lost a book. She looked inside to find her own small jump starter. Picking up the card she read,

These are very handy and I thought maybe you could use one with your old jalopy. Max.

With a smile, she quickly stashed the device in her drawer so the teachers wouldn't know what she'd received. They didn't need to know who had left her a nice surprise. A surprise, that even though it was a gadget, warmed her inside and made her happy.

Later that morning, she went to the lounge for coffee, and he was there pouring himself a cup. Glancing around, she made certain that Kevin McBride, the science teacher, was not there before she entered.

"Are you looking for someone?"

She shook her head. "I'm checking to make certain someone is not here."

"Oh," he said. "Me?"

"Not you," she said with a laugh, but thought that would've probably been a good idea. Maybe then her attention span would return to normal.

"Who?"

"If you must know, I try to avoid Kevin McBride."

He grinned.

"I have my reasons," she said.

"Like what?"

"Oh, he's clingy and doesn't take no for an answer. Every week he asks me out and every week, I say no. He's persistent."

"Understood," he acknowledged with a laugh.

"Thanks for the booster."

"You're welcome. Driving that old car, a booster is necessary. When are you going to purchase a vehicle made in this century?"

"Hey, it's not that old."

"The junkyard is missing Grandma's ole Buick."

"When I'm no longer on a teacher's salary, I'll buy a new one," she said.

He laughed. "Pitiful."

"Shut up, Mr. Corvette."

"Yes, ma'am, Miss Junker. What time did you get home last night?"

"Not too bad. The mechanic took about thirty minutes to switch out the old battery and charge the new one. It was almost six when I walked through the door. Last night was my advanced science, algorithms class. I'm not certain I'm going to pass."

For the last week, she was having trouble studying and felt distracted. Since she'd done that stupid Cupid dance, she wasn't concentrating well and it was no one's fault but her own.

"Why is that?"

"Because the math is complicated and when you combine scientific research, programming, and numbers, it's easy to become confused."

She wasn't about to say because a certain coach had picked her up naked on the side of the road, sparking all kinds of interest again. She refused to admit that was part of the reason for her lack of focus.

Taking a Styrofoam cup, he poured coffee and handed it to her. "I've been thinking. Since I helped you last night, I think you owe me another night on the town."

"Oh no. Every time you help me in some way I have to go out with you?"

"No, it would be simpler if you'd just agree we should date again," he said matter-of-factly. "I don't like fighting though."

"Good, neither do I. So it's resolved. We're not going out again."

A grin spread across his face. "That's what you're saying now."

OPENING THE DOOR, Meghan entered the teacher's lounge and glanced around. If possible, she tried to eat her lunch either in her car or outside, but today the north wind blew and the winter months made that impossible.

Most often during her free period when she visited the lounge, Max was holding court. Today when she walked in, only five teachers sat eating, and one of them was known for spreading gossip. Quickly, she took the only empty table, praying no one would notice her while she dined alone.

Mr. Googly Eyes McBride, the science teacher resided at another table devouring his ham on rye sandwich that he ate every day.

Meghan loved nerds, but this man exuded false intelligence and dressed in his father's seventy's bell bottoms. A nice man, just not someone she wanted to date. The entire year, it seemed he could not take the hint she wasn't interested, not even a little.

"Meghan, how goes the library?" he asked, moving to sit beside her.

"Hi, Kevin," she said. "The library is busy with seniors working on their final term papers."

Another teacher came through the door, laughing and talking on her cell phone.

She would need to cut her time short and return to her desk or be bombarded with Kevin's flirtatious dumbness until it reached a crescendo where he would ask her if she'd like to go to the movies with him Friday night. This scenario had been played out several times already and listening to him pontificate his brilliance was like nails scratching against a hard surface. Irritating.

"Yeah, that time of year. Got any great plans for the summer? I'm going on a cruise," he said. "A singles cruise."

"That's wonderful," she said, knowing instinctively what his next words were going to be.

"I was thinking, hey, you're unmarried, I'm unmarried. What if we went on this singles cruise together," he said as Max walked in the door.

McBride certainly didn't waste any time throwing out a net trying to reel her in. The man was relentless to say the least.

The expression on her face must have clued Max in that she was in trouble. That mischievous grin she once fell in love with overcoming his face. "Meghan, I was looking for you. What time do you want me to pick you up Saturday morning? We should get an early start."

Her lips pressed together in a frown. They had no plans for Saturday morning. Sure, Max had been pressuring her to go out with him again, but nothing was confirmed. Maybe she owed him one for helping with her car, buying her the new battery charger, but she hadn't agreed to anything. Then again...if it got rid of Googly Eyes.

"How about eight o'clock. What are we doing?"

Max grinned and she knew he'd found a breach in her defense and was running down the field for the touchdown. "It's a surprise."

Kevin looked between the two of them. "You're dating the coach?"

The self-confident jock smiled at the teacher and let the nerd know she was a useless opportunity for him to pursue. "We dated back in high school. You weren't here then, but our classmates called us the M&M couple. Now we've returned, and well, I couldn't resist her. So we're seeing each other again. Who knows where this will lead."

She tried to make him stop, glaring at him. She couldn't believe he was blathering their past in front of everyone. The rumor mill would be abuzz, whispering M&M were back. What could she do?

Call him out, and face Kevin's attempts at comfort every day? A twinge of pity came over her as the dejected man stared at her in shock. A disgusted glower radiated from Kevin's eyes like he didn't believe she would go out with a coach over him.

"We've gone out once since he came back," she said quietly.

"And now we're going out again," Max responded.

"I guess the singles cruise is out," Kevin said dejectedly.

"Sorry, I'm attending classes all summer."

"Oh, by the way, I signed us up to help organize the spring dance and also to be class sponsors for Seniors next year," Max said with a grin, knowing he was causing trouble.

"You did what?" she said, frustration mounting.

"They needed help, and well, we work so well together, I thought you wouldn't mind."

Closing her eyes, she sighed. She went to school four days a week. She didn't have time to be a sponsor.

Right now, she wanted to commit murder. She wanted to hurt Max for making them a spectacle in the teacher's lounge. And for signing them up as sponsors of the senior class. Yet, a tiny part of her felt giddy they were going on another date.

AT FOUR O'CLOCK, Meghan walked through the door of Taylor's restaurant, her curly hair straight, dark circles under her eyes, her mouth pursed in a frown. Who said being a librarian was easy? After today, Meghan and Max were the hot topic around school. Trending even more than the Basketball Queen.

"I need a root beer float," she said, sinking down at one of the tables. Her life was in such turmoil right now with Max pursuing her, her studies and her job. She needed something that would make her feel good, if only for a moment.

"Coming right up," Taylor said, disappearing into the kitchen.

A few minutes later, Taylor placed the floats on the table. "Tough day?"

"Since Coach Max rescued my naked ass, he thinks we should do all these school events together. As in organizing the spring dance next month. Crowning the Basketball Queen and now he volunteered us as Senior sponsors for next year. He's crawled up my butt so far, he'll need a flashlight to find his way out."

Taylor started giggling.

"You shouldn't be laughing. This is all your fault."

"You two have been dancing around each other for months. The Cupid incident brought it all out in the open."

Until he picked her up nude, she had been able to avoid him most of the time. But now it was getting harder to stay away from the big handsome hunk of man.

"Well, I would have preferred to sweep Max and our history under the rug. I don't want to deal with the professional jock itch."

"Call his bluff. See if he really will tell the school board about the other night."

Max would never threaten to tell the school board. He hadn't even mentioned telling anyone after he picked her up that Friday night. But to let everyone in school know they were dating, she almost felt like he'd put a "keep out" sign on her.

"It's not that. Max would never expose me. It's just...I told him the science teacher, Mr. Googly Eyes McBride, has been clingy and doesn't take no for an answer. So today in the teacher's lounge, right in front of the scientist, Max asked what time should he pick me up Saturday morning."

"Did the science nerd get the message?" Taylor asked.

"Yes, it solved my problem with Googly Eyes McBride. More

than half the teachers in school were in the lounge eating lunch and now Max and I are the gossips' latest buzz."

"Wow, one problem solved, another created."

"Yeah, I feel like I'm wearing a sumo wrestler outfit and we're bouncing against one another. I'm scared to death there will be Velcro somewhere and we'll stick."

"Do you want me to put on a sumo outfit and you can practice with me?"

Her brows raised and she giggled. "You're nuts."

"Drink your root beer; it will calm you."

"Thanks," she said, "but I may need something stronger."

They sat, drinking floats, letting peace settle over her.

"What can you tell me about Kelsey and Ryan's break-up?"

"Good grief," Meghan said. "We're all back in Cupid. Sometimes I wake up and think we've returned to high school. Are we in a time warp?"

"No," Taylor said, shaking her head. "You're a librarian. I'm a cook."

"Don't make me rethink my career decision," Meghan said, tossing her auburn hair. "After days like today, being a rocket scientist might have been easier."

"I know," Taylor responded.

"What happened between Ryan and Kelsey?"

Meghan frowned at her over her root beer.

"Something went wrong right after we graduated at an end of year party, but I don't know what. Her family whisked her out of town and took her on an expensive vacation to Italy as a graduation present. We didn't speak again for years," Meghan said. "Sorry, I guess I wasn't much help. Why are you asking?"

"Oh, I wondered what happened to the two of them. She hates him."

Meghan's eyes grew wide and she put her spoon down, cursing beneath her breath. "Oh no. You're dating him."

Taylor vigorously shook her head. "No. No, I'm not."

Meghan sat across the table staring at her. "For some reason, I don't believe you."

"No, Ryan and I are not seeing each other."

That's what Taylor was telling herself, but Meghan thought differently. She'd been terribly interested in Ryan since the night of the Cupid dance. Could she be falling for Ryan? That was like asking if Meghan was falling for Max all over again. No, no, no...she refused.

§.

AT SUNRISE SATURDAY MORNING, he picked up Meghan, and once again, she brought out her overnight bag. Inside her condo, she looked beautiful in her jeans. Unable to resist, he gave her a quick peck on the lips.

Nothing like what he hoped to do with her tonight, just a nice reminder of what they shared.

"Are you ready?"

"Yes," she said breathlessly. "What are we doing?"

"It's a surprise. But you're going to love it."

He helped her into the Corvette and three hours later, they arrived at DFW airport in Dallas where they were whisked on board a small private airplane.

"Good grief, I can't believe we're flying in a jet."

"Relax, we'll be there soon, and after that, the fun begins. By the way, I hope you're okay with us not getting back until late tomorrow. We have separate room reservations at the hotel."

If only he could persuade her to share his room. Then they could wake up together. He knew he was rushing things, but he couldn't help himself.

"Sure," she said. "As long as we're back to school on Monday."

"Can't miss. Tryouts for varsity start next week."

"You really love football, don't you?"

"Yes," he said, perplexed. "You didn't realize that all those years ago?"

"Of course, I did. But I thought you would grow out of it. After you quit playing professional ball, I thought you would find something else. You're still in the game, only this time helping kids."

In almost every football player's life, there was a coach who encouraged and boosted the kid to the next level.

His coach had been the one who first told him if he continued and didn't get injured, there was a chance he would go professional. And he had. All the way through college, he'd worked hard, done what the coaches wanted, trained, eaten right, ignored the partying and in the end, been rewarded when he'd gone in the third round of the draft. Then he'd partied.

"I feel blessed to play ball for as many years as I did before I got hurt. Football is in my blood and I want to encourage other young men to work hard and get into professional ball. That's what you do. Help others climb the ladder and continue the game."

Shaking her head, she seemed bewildered. "You were a sweet kid in school, but I like the older version of you even more."

"Good."

"So what are we doing today? You've been so mysterious."

"We're attending the science and engineering festival in DC."

"Oh my God. Not the national one with all the companies exhibiting and talking about their latest inventions."

"That's the one," he said with a grin. "When I checked the schedule, NASA, Homeland Security, the Department of Defense, Lockheed Martin, all will be there with an exhibit and some will be doing demonstrations."

She reached across the aisle and grabbed his hand. "Oh, I've wanted to attend this for so long and never had the opportunity." She placed her hands on his head, pulled him to her and kissed him softly on the lips. "Thank you."

"If I'd known you would react that way, we would have flown out yesterday."

With a quick glance at her watch, she smiled. "I can't wait."

"We'll spend the night at the convention hotel. We'll have access to the show as long as it's open."

When he made the reservations, he asked for two rooms with connecting doors, but planned to convince her to stay with him. If not, at least maybe they could dine together in her room.

Still, in time, he hoped to finally persuade her to talk about the past.

All he needed was closure. To understand why she didn't want their child and put this behind him, then he could move on.

He'd never told a soul what had broken them up. Only his mother understood how deeply betrayed he felt and tried to tell him things always worked out like they should.

He didn't think so. Max and Meghan should have married. Their son or daughter should be with them right now.

Funny how he hadn't perceived when he prepared this trip what would be her reaction. Memories of the women he dated during his pro days swept over him, and with a laugh, he knew not one would step through the door of a science fair.

Meghan was different, she was the other half of the M&Ms and he liked the fact she wasn't just a pretty face looking to hook up or boost her modeling career dating a pro ball player.

Finding something he thought she would enjoy had been challenging. He thought she would like getting away from school and seeing some exhibits in an area she was interested in.

Now he knew exactly what would make her happy. Not too many women were excited in a grownup science fair.

CHAPTER 5

*M*eghan couldn't remember the last time she had so much fun. She'd visited with several of the vendors and one had even told her to contact him when she received her doctorate. They were always looking for candidates.

Her feet ached, she just wanted to put her pajamas on, collapse on the bed and watch a few minutes of mindless TV before she passed out asleep.

Frowning, she noticed Max arguing with the registration clerk at the front desk. Curious, Meghan leaned forward to hear what he was saying.

"My assistant said she reserved two rooms with a connecting door. Look, I have the confirmation numbers."

"I'm sorry, sir, but the hotel is overbooked. There is only one room left if you want that or you're going to need to find another place to stay."

He gave a little laugh. "You don't understand. She's not going to believe I didn't do this on purpose. What about a rollaway? Is there one available?"

Oh my God, her chest ached as she realized they were out of

rooms. They were going to have to share. Unless they left the hotel, she would have to sleep in the same bed as Max. Heat flooded her center and she swallowed. This didn't mean they had to have sex. This only meant there was one room.

The woman punched something into her computer and glanced back up at him. "We're out of rollaways. With the fair going, we're at full capacity tonight."

"Explain that to my..."

The desk clerk raised her brows and Max shook his head. "Never mind. We'll take the room."

"Good," the woman said and quickly processed the key handing it to him. "Enjoy your stay."

Walking toward Meghan, she pretended to look through the exhibit's brochure. When he walked up, she gazed at him. "Problems?"

"Yes. I have a confirmation for two rooms, but we were lucky to get one."

"That's convenient. Are you sleeping in the car?"

"Hardly," he said. "It's DC. We can try to find another hotel if you'd like."

Shaking her head. "Oh, no. Tomorrow, I want to hit that last exhibit. The one about life on other planets."

That would mean she would be forced to sleep in the same room as Max.

"No rollaways?"

"All gone."

"How about I'll spend the night on the floor and you can have the bed."

"Absolutely not," he said. "I'll sleep on the floor."

"No. You're not," she replied, gazing at him, realizing they were drawing attention standing in the lobby discussing where they would stay. "Your football injuries don't need a hard carpet."

"Let's go check out the room."

Placing his hand on her back, he guided her toward the elevators away from the people staring at them. His heart was pounding inside his chest. This was what he wanted, and yet, now that he had the opportunity, it didn't feel right.

When they arrived at the concierge level, they pulled their suitcases in the room and looked around. A king size bed sat in the center of the room.

Meghan walked over and sank onto the mattress. Exhausted, she didn't know if she would ever rise again. She laid down. "Do you promise to be a gentleman?"

"I'm too tired to be anything but a gentleman."

"Good, me too. What if we just put a rolled-up blanket between us. You sleep on your side and I'll rest on my side." Gazing at him, he walked over and sat down beside her. "No talking at school about how we spent the night together."

Laughing, he shook his head. "I'd be too embarrassed to admit I took a fellow teacher to a hotel and all I could do was sleep."

Tired beyond caring, she grinned at him. "Could we put on our PJs, order room service, and rest?"

"Sounds like a wonderful plan."

"Then, let's do it."

Later than night, a sense of peace overcame Max. On the other side of the bed, Meghan lay in her pajamas. Max wore a pair of workout shorts and a T-shirt. Together they reclined in bed with a blanket between them. It seemed like the perfect end to a perfect day.

The television had been on and they watched the weather and then she pulled up the covers and closed her eyes. Reaching over to the nightstand, he turned off the TV.

Reaching over the makeshift bundling board, he took her hand. "Goodnight, Meghan. Sweet dreams."

"Night, Max. And thank you for today. I had such a great time."

His heart warmed and he would have liked nothing better

than to roll over and pull her into his arms. But he didn't want to scare her. "You're welcome."

THE NEXT MORNING, Meghan awoke to the feel of a hard male body wrapped around her. His arm lay across her stomach and the two of them snuggled deeply in the covers. This wasn't supposed to happen. Yet, being in his arms felt so good, lying in bed with him, waking to the scent of a man.

Meghan was trying not to be affected by him, but he kept doing things that made her happy. He'd always been a great guy, just one who put sports and football and his team ahead of her. When she thought she was pregnant, he hadn't even called. But rather disappeared from the planet for three days. Finally, when he didn't respond to her texts, she couldn't handle the silence any longer.

By that time, she found out the supposed child was nothing more than a scare. Probably because of the uncertainty in her life and all the stress of graduating high school, preparing for college and everything changing around her. During that brief time, she had been truly frightened.

The thought of a baby at eighteen was more than she could fathom. And yet she would have learned to manage if the pregnancy had been real. Other women went to school after having a child and she would have coped.

"Morning," he said in her ear.

"Good morning," she whispered. "What happened to the blanket."

He laughed. "Honestly, I didn't touch it. When I awoke this morning, the bundle was gone. Sometime last night, I got cold and with no blanket on the bed, I went in search of warmth."

"Looks like you found it," she said, her voice husky at his touch. This felt so right and she didn't want to move.

"Feels pretty darn nice," he responded, kissing the side of her neck.

A shiver went through her and all the old fears rushed at her like a freight train. She wasn't on the pill. Had no need to be on birth control, yet they were in bed together, with him caressing her neck. She must get away to clear her head. If she did this, he would hurt her again and she refused to give him a second chance at breaking her heart.

"Time to rise and shine," she said, throwing back the covers. "We should shower, eat breakfast, and get over to the convention when they open at nine. What time is our flight?"

Jumping out of bed, she glanced back at him as she gathered her clothing. The cool air hit her and she missed the warmth of Max's body. The feel of him curled around her, the strength of his embrace.

"We can leave any time, but I told the pilot two."

"Then let's get rolling," she said, hurrying into the bathroom.

Max rolled over and let out a heavy sigh. "I must be a masochist."

"What?"

"Nothing. Hurry, I'm going to need in there or we could share the shower, which would take less time."

Meghan quickly locked the door. One caress, and they would be right back to the way they were before, only this time they would be older, a little wiser, and so much more vulnerable.

THE PLANE TOOK off at five p.m. He glanced at Meghan. Sitting back, she looked out the window at the sparkling glitter of DC.

"It's a beautiful city," he said, seeing the lights flickering below them.

"Yes, I can't tell you how much fun I had this weekend. This was wonderful. Thank you," she said. "Several companies gave me their cards and want me to contact them when I'm ready to intern." With a sigh, she smiled at him.

All day, he watched her almost running from booth to booth, talking to people, consuming the information from their exhibit. The elation on her face had been like observing a child. Her giddiness made his insides heat, making him happy that he brought her here and let her experience something he held no interest in.

"That was the best date I've ever been on," she said laughing. "You topped them all."

Reaching out he took her hand. "I'm glad you enjoyed yourself."

"It must be nice to afford all this," she said pointing to the plane. "You could have taken me bowling or to the movies and I would have been happy, but this...you're going to make it hard for any other man to top your date."

"That was my plan." He squeezed her hand. "Don't want another man to show you a better time than me," he said with a grin.

"Professional football helped you so much financially, but I saw you get hurt on television. I saw the pain and wanted to go down there and tackle that defensive lineman for injuring you."

"The player was only doing his job. It was a clean hit, just in the wrong place. Tore my ACL. At that point, it was the third time and the doc said it's over. Time to call it quits."

Shocked she hadn't pulled away, he continued to hold her hand. He liked the feel of her skin touching his, loved waking up next to her this morning and hoped that maybe, it would go further. But she jumped out of bed quicker than a strike from a rattlesnake.

Gazing at him, he could see the sympathy that radiated from her warm emerald eyes. "As much as you love football, how did you take the news."

Those days had been a horrible time in his life. A time he

knew would eventually appear, but he'd wanted to play a few more years. Unfortunately, retirement arrived faster than he expected.

"Depressed. Being injured, I went into a deep depression. My mother was so worried, she flew out to Minnesota where I'd been hurt and we came home together. Mom stayed a week, helping me, cooking my favorite meals and talking to me about the next chapter in my life."

"But high school football?"

Though he loved the small town of Cupid, he knew it was a stepping stone to something bigger. Yet, he loved his high school. That was where it all began for him and he was showing young players how to succeed at the game. He loved his job. Now if only he could get his personal life in order.

"First, I went to work for a trainer, hoping to help him with his NFL recruits. Training them how to be better, but that's not what I love about the game. For one year, I trained athletes before I understood I missed the excitement, the suspense, the plays. I realized I wanted to spend my time teaching young kids the game of football. So I started looking for a coaching position."

That first year had been tough. Kind of reminded him of his first year of college. A new environment, learning new techniques, new plays, with no one to share the frustration and the excitement. Missing Meghan.

"And here you are."

"For now. A couple of years here and then I will be going to a college team. Or at least, I hope I will be."

The airplane hit a pocket of turbulence and the cabin bounced a little. She held on tighter to his hand, shivering. "Sorry, I hate turbulence. I know flying is safer than driving, but still, I like a smooth ride with an easy landing."

Part of him longed to ask her about the past, but they'd had such a great time together, he didn't want to spoil the atmosphere. Wanting only to continue to enjoy her company, her laughter, her smile, her intelligence. He wasn't a dummy by any means, but Meghan's IQ was a few points higher than his own. She would be the doctor and he would be the coach.

Shaking his head at the thought, for the first time he wondered if he could forgive her for what she'd done to their child. Could they have a second chance at happiness?

CHAPTER 6

A week passed and while he'd seen glimpses of Meghan, she'd been standoffish. She hadn't been in the teacher's lounge and every time he went to the library, she was either in a meeting or helping a student. No matter what he did, she was unavailable.

The weekend trip had been wonderful and now he missed her. Today was tough and he wanted to see her. He wanted to talk about the past and learn if somehow they could move forward or end it once and for all. Before his heart became so involved, he couldn't walk away.

Without calling, he drove the Corvette to her home. Knocking on the door, he wondered if she would open to him.

Just then the door swung wide and she smiled. As always, she looked gorgeous in her yoga pants, T-shirt, and tennis shoes. Auburn curls spilled from a clip on top of her head, and his fingers ached to tangle in her hair.

"Hey," he said. "Are you on your way to work out?"

"Nope. Just got back. My weekly yoga class. What are you doing?"

Motioning for him to come inside, he walked through the

door. "I'm restless. The weather finally warmed up, and well, let's go walking. Come with me? I need some company."

Though he sounded desperate, the second date had showed him he still enjoyed her company. There could even still be feelings for her. Maybe he was crazy for caring, but he needed to understand what had happened in the past before he could trust her to move forward into the future. He either needed closure or to consider pursuing a life together. He wasn't certain which.

"Okay, let me grab a jacket," she said. "Tonight, I planned to study, but it would be nice to go for a walk."

"I'll even buy you a hamburger."

"That's a temptation a girl can't turn down," she grabbed a lightweight coat and headed out the door.

Helping her into the Corvette, the urge to return to their favorite spot overwhelmed him. Soon they were speeding toward the hiking trails of their youth. The lake where they spent a lot of time making out in the car. Discovering each other's body, exploring nature, and talking about the future.

"Why are you restless?"

"One of my kids, my best player got into trouble. His college scholarship will be yanked so fast, he won't see it coming. The sad part is he doesn't know why everyone is upset. The poor kid doesn't understand what he's done." With a quick glance at her, he asked, "Were we that stupid?"

Today when he learned that his student had been arrested for being drunk on public property and possession of alcohol, he'd been so torn. The kid had a bright future, but not if he continued on this path.

"Probably. At that time, we didn't realize the consequences of not following the rules and the lasting effects."

"Is that what happened with us?"

"Too young, that's what happened to us," she said. "Raging hormones, two kids not realizing the dangers."

"Your dad cautioned us."

"Yes, but parents don't believe their children are going to have sex. When it happened, we weren't prepared."

Back then, the tension between them had been building for months and the night it happened, it turned into a celebration that culminated with them sharing the most intimate act on earth. He had no regrets about that night.

Automatically, he drove his car to the oak tree where years before they had made out in his car. Putting the car in park, he hopped out and came around to help her.

"Let's walk that trail along the edge of the water."

"It's going to be dark soon," she warned.

"If we get lost, we'll have to stay the night."

"Not happening," she said. "We'll find our way back."

Taking her hand, they began to stroll the path, stepping over rocks. "Brings back a lot of memories."

"Yes," she said, glancing away, not looking in his eyes.

"Do you remember the night the team made the playoffs?"

That night was a sweet dream. Not only had his team won a place in the division showdown, but his girl and him had experienced a night of sweetness he would never forget. One that still made him ache when he thought of the love the two of them shared.

"How could I forget. The whole town was so excited. Between the newspaper and the Dallas news station interviewing you, I thought we'd never arrive at the celebration party." Gazing at him, she sighed. "After dating our entire senior year, everyone thought we would marry."

"Both of us wanted to attend college."

"Yes, we did," she replied. "Our parents were right to insist that we give each other time to figure out what we wanted."

Squeezing her hand, his voice rough, he said, "They didn't have to worry. We broke up before we left."

"It was for the best," she responded.

Part of him wanted to scream, no it wasn't for the best. It had taken him his entire freshman year of college before he'd become interested in girls again. And even then, it was only because his buddies were giving him hell for not dating.

A moment of silence passed as they continued walking the path along the edge of the lake.

"You are probably the person I've dated the longest. My only other serious relationship lasted about three months. Until he learned I was going to pursue my education and receive my doctorate. Maybe he was a little intimidated by the fact I would have a higher degree than him."

"What was his bachelors in?"

"Accounting," she said with a snort. "Really dull stuff."

"The idea that you enjoy science as much as you do fascinates me. How many women like to watch an experiment on different chemical components and observe their reaction? Going to the fair, I finally understood why you love science. Honestly, I can tell you I'd be bored in no time."

"I love it," she said softly.

"As much as I hate to say this, we should head back to the car."

"I'd forgotten how much I liked walking this path. This has been so enjoyable. Now that spring is on the way, let's come out and do this again."

The word rippled down his spine. It was the first time she'd mentioned doing something together, the two of them. No, it wasn't much, it wasn't a promise of a date, but it was a start.

"Any time," he said his voice husky and deep, filled with the emotions of the past.

The sun sank beneath the horizon, leaving them in the twilight as they hurried back. In the darkness, rustling came from the bushes as animals bedded down for the night.

When they reached the covered picnic table where he had parked the car, he helped her onto the top where they sat and gazed. The moon had risen and the light shimmered over the rippling water.

Max stared at the lake where he spent so many years swimming, fishing, boating and growing up. Someday he hoped his own children would play here.

"Do you remember what occurred here," she asked.

Oh yes, he remembered how they came here after the big game. Memories of the first time they made love overcame him. Two fumbling teenagers learning about desire. Then they came back in March and again in April and... again when their child had been conceived. Though they used condoms, they both were aware of the risks of her getting pregnant.

And then one night the condom ripped.

"Yes, I remember."

A sarcastic laugh bubbled from her. "What girl gives a boy her virginity at the lake on a picnic table?"

Pulling her close, his voice husky with the emotions this place evoked. "A very special girl."

Could they talk about that memorable time between them? If only he could stare into her gaze to witness her feelings, but the dark shadowed her eyes. "A girl I thought I would spend forever with."

Leaning her head toward him, he captured her mouth with his. Kissing her, his lips plundered hers, his tongue sliding between her teeth, dancing and twirling with her own as the kiss turned demanding and fiery. Laying her back onto the table, his mouth consumed her. A kiss from the past transported to today.

Fueled with passion, he recalled how they expressed their longing the first time right here.

Headlights turned down the road and a group of kids went by yelling and screaming out the window as they drove by.

Jerking apart, he stared at her in amazement. All these years later, the emotions still existed just below the surface.

Her breathing was heavy, her lips swollen as she smiled at him. "Your car is easily recognized. Maybe you should buy me that burger you promised."

Max was famished, but it wasn't for food. No, he wanted to continue the exploration of her mouth, he wanted to continue seducing her, he wanted to begin again, right where they left off.

Sighing, he knew she was right. Now was not the time and while this had been an excellent place years ago, it no longer seemed quite as appealing.

"You're right. Let's get some food."

But when he took her home...hopefully she would feed his real hunger.

MAX TURNED onto the highway out of the burger joint near the lake and headed the Corvette back to Cupid. They were about fifteen minutes from town. Far enough the ordinance against liquor no longer applied. Two busy stores sat right at the county line.

Tonight, they'd made a little progress talking about the past. Remembering the good times, avoiding the touchy subjects of their breakup. And yet, he still didn't have the closure he needed. He still had to understand why she broke up with him.

Sure, he hadn't responded to her text messages. While away at football camp, he made the decision not to react, but rather think about their future and how they would handle the pregnancy.

When he walked into the first session, he'd been stunned as they picked up everyone's phone. The coach insisting there would be no distractions while they learned the plays. As soon as they returned the phones, he immediately tried to contact her via texts, phone calls. But she never answered his calls again.

"The first time I went away to college, the coaches took our cell phones away. After I check with the administration, I'm thinking of doing that to my kids when they come to training."

She gazed at him. "What are you talking about?"

Cars sped past them on the highway, their headlights shining.

The two-lane road was dark and winding as they headed toward Cupid.

"The very first football camp I attended, they took our phones when we entered the room. The coaches kept them until the last day of camp. It was the summer we broke up."

In the cramped quarters of the Corvette, he felt her tense.

"What do you think Principal Jones would think of me taking my students' phones away. That way I have their undivided attention. Otherwise, I'm competing with their friends, family, girlfriends and video games. Their brain is occupied with answering their texts and not on my game preparation."

"We have the same problem. Some kids just come in to make calls or to text. My new rule is if I don't see a book or a textbook and the student working, they will be asked to leave. The library is not a phone lounge."

With a subtle nudge, he was trying to let her know why he never responded to her texts all those years ago. Sure, he texted her explaining he just got his phone back, but the silence was heartbreaking.

But he didn't know if she received the message or had been so angry, she ignored his text, his voice mails. Or even worse, she blocked him.

Even today, if she realized what he was saying, she gave him no indication she understood. No matter how he tried, she refused to discuss the past.

Maybe she read his message and decided to ignore him. Obviously, he wasn't going to be able to be subtle in his approach to learning the truth.

"Max?" she said, her voice strained.

Staring out the windshield, he couldn't believe what he was seeing. Headlights glowed on his side of the road headed toward them. Flashing his lights, they didn't slow down. The car weaved into the ditch alongside the road, then shot back onto the highway in their lane.

With oncoming traffic, there was no place for him to avoid the errant car. He had nowhere to dodge this fool driving right at them. He had no choice.

Turning the wheel and slamming on the brakes, he heard Meghan screaming, "Max."

The impact was on his side of the Corvette and he dreamed he was back playing football, except this time, instead of hitting hard flesh, he hit the doorframe. The air bags deployed and blackness overcame him.

§

MEGHAN MOVED INSIDE THE CORVETTE, pushing the air bag away, releasing her seat belt. Shock pulsing through her, making her slow and cautious. In a daze, she glanced around the car. Max lay slumped against the seat, a breeze came in where once there had been a window. The front quarter panel of the Corvette twisted at an odd angle. The other vehicle smashed against where the wheel should have been.

"Max," she questioned. Shaking his shoulder. He didn't move. "Max."

The screams welled up inside her and she screamed his name over and over, her heart pounding in her chest, but he didn't respond. She needed to call for help. Where was her purse, her phone?

Dear God, he was injured.

As if in a dream, she reached over and turned the Corvette off, in case any gas leaked, fearful of a fire. Someone knocked on her side, causing her to jump.

"Are you all right?"

Opening the door, she gazed at the man, still not certain this was real. "Call an ambulance. My friend is not responding."

Moving in a sluggish motion, she couldn't believe this was not a delusion. Staring between the spider webbed cracks of the windshield at the other car, she saw the front end now sat in the driver's seat. How could they have survived?

Glancing down, she checked to see if she was bleeding, but nothing hurt. The air bags had protected her with the biggest impact on Max's side of the car.

Fear consumed her, Max lay unmoving, his body collapsed against the curved seat of the car he loved.

Frightened of doing more damage to him, she didn't dare move him, but she couldn't leave him either. Tears filled her eyes. "Oh, Max, you've got to be all right. Stay with me, Max."

Was he even alive? With trembling hands, she felt for his heartbeat on his neck. A steady rhythm pound beneath her fingertips and she sighed with relief. At least he was still with her. Laying her hand on his chest, his lungs rose and fell.

And then she saw the blood trickling down his forehead.

The urge to get out and kick the other driver's ass was strong. He'd either been passing or driving on the wrong side of the road.

The stranger was back at the door, talking to her--but she felt like she was in a well.

"Ma'am, an ambulance is on the way. What about you? Are you hurt?"

"I'm fine, but my friend, he's not moving or waking up. He's got a pulse and he's breathing, but he's unconscious," she said, her eyes tearing up.

What if he never woke up? What if the memories he wanted to discuss never reached closure for either of them? What if she never had the chance to kiss him again?

A sob escaped and she wiped the moisture away. "Talk to me, Max. I need you to speak to me. Let me know you're okay."

In the distance, she could hear sirens wailing, but she couldn't move from his side. Until he opened those big brown eyes of his, she wasn't moving.

"Max, this is not how our story ends. Do you understand me.

You're not leaving me now. You did that years ago, but this time you're not leaving me like this. Damn you. Now wake up and talk to me."

Silence echoed in the car. Suddenly the door opened and Ryan Jones pulled her from the vehicle.

CHAPTER 7

$\mathcal{M}$eghan didn't want to leave the car with Max inside, but Ryan gave her no choice.

"Let me stay with him," she insisted.

"You're in the way of the paramedics. Until they can secure him, they won't move him. Let them do their job."

He was right. But still she feared Max would take his last breath and she wouldn't be there beside him.

Together, they watched the EMTs work on getting Max out of the wrecked vehicle. They strapped a C-collar around his neck, making certain moving him would not cause more damage while another man took his vital signs.

Unable to get his door open, they used the Jaws of Life to remove the metal to reach Max.

Trembles racked her body when she gazed at the truck where the officials had placed a drape over the body of the person who hit them. Wrapping a blanket around her, Ryan stood beside her staring at the rescuers.

"You're sure you're all right?" Ryan questioned, his gaze flickering over her. "When we get to the ER you should be checked out."

Tomorrow she would probably be sore, but right now, her concern was Max.

"The airbags deployed and saved me. That driver was on the wrong side of the road. Why did Max turn the car in his direction," she asked, shocked. "The brunt of the impact was on his side."

In the night air, Ryan's radio crackled something. One deputy was directing traffic, while another was taking pictures and writing up notes.

"I suspect he was trying to protect you. Probably, realized there was nothing he could do to stop the accident and turned the wheel to save you."

A chill went through her as tears welled up in her eyes. She was not injured because of Max's selfless act. She swallowed the tears in her throat.

"The driver of the other vehicle must have passed out. The smell of alcohol was strong. You're both lucky to be alive. Now, I only pray Max is not too terribly injured."

"He's still out cold. I know he's breathing and he has a pulse," she said, staring at the Corvette, wishing they would see some kind of movement from Max.

As they stood watching the paramedics load Max onto a gurney, her heart pounded in her chest. Quickly, they rolled him to the waiting ambulance.

Glancing around the scene, Ryan sighed. "My deputies are working the accident. Come on, we'll follow the EMTs and then I'll come back and help them."

"Thanks," Meghan said, knowing she didn't want to be far from Max. As soon as they arrived at the hospital and she knew more about his condition, she'd call his mother.

Climbing into the patrol car, Ryan turned his lights and siren on and followed the ambulance into town. It all seemed surreal and Meghan had to fight the urge to cry.

"Had Max been drinking?"

With a laugh, she shook her head. While many professional football players had DUIs, her man, Max didn't even like to drink.

"Only if you consider root beer floats an alcoholic beverage. Max worries about driving on the road with drunks. Now I understand why. And his car. He loved that car and is going to be so upset."

"Was he speeding?"

"No. Max always worries about other drivers. And yet, he gets hit."

Shaking his head, Ryan sighed. "During the last three months, that's the third fatality on this stretch of highway. I'm going to have my officers set up a sting for drunks. We'll fill the jail the first hour we conduct sobriety tests."

"Scary," she replied, her focus on the EMT wagon, her thinking still fuzzy. "So you think the reason Max turned the car was to protect me?"

"Yes," Ryan answered. "The investigator will measure Max's skid marks, but it appears he saw the truck and spun the Corvette sideways. The left front side of the car, looks like a bomb exploded. If you slam head on, there might have been more than one body bag tonight."

A sick nausea filled her stomach at how close they'd come to being killed.

"Maybe I don't want to go out to dinner at the lake on Friday nights. Maybe I just want to stay home."

"It's best to be off the roads between eleven p.m. and four a.m.," he said glancing at her.

"But it's only nine," Meghan protested.

"You're right. You guys managed to find one of the early drunks."

The transport pulled up in the emergency entrance. After parking the sheriff's car in a reserved spot, the two jumped out, almost running to the swishing doors of the ER.

By the time they reached the door, they had wheeled Max into an exam room.

Meghan wanted to go in, but knew hospital regulations would forbid it unless he asked for her. She wasn't his wife. She wasn't even his next of kin. She was only the girl who had loved him for years and still did.

Tears swelled in her eyes. She did love him. Even after all the heartbreak, seven years later, she still loved her Max.

WITH A GASP, Max woke, trying to rise off the gurney.

"What the hell? Where is Meghan?" he demanded staring up at the medical professional.

"Calm down. She's all right," the paramedic told him. "We're concerned about you. Looks like your head hit the window."

"I'm fine," he said, though his head pounded and he recognized the signs. Had experienced them in football more times than he wished to remember. Concussion. After a while, he learned to diagnose himself.

"Pupils are dilated," a nurse called out in a calm no-nonsense voice. "Blood pressure is high, but stable. Pulse is steady."

The paramedics slid the backboard onto the bed. A collar was around his neck and he tried to rise, but quickly realized he was strapped down. Where was Meghan? Why wasn't she by his side? Was she truly all right or were they lying to him?

"Where's my girlfriend?" he asked.

His mind flashed back to the accident. The last thing he remembered was truck headlights coming straight at them. On the two-lane road, there was no place for him to go.

"Any tingling or numbness?"

"None. I want to go home," he replied. "Where is Meghan?"

The second paramedic opened the door and glanced out. "A pretty redhead with curly hair is talking to the sheriff."

"That's Meghan. Tell her to come here," he insisted.

"Sorry, there's not enough room and we need to finish checking you out," the nurse said. "The doctor should be coming in the door any second."

"No, I'm not staying the night," Max told the woman. With football injuries, he had been in enough hospitals to know you never got any rest and they were nothing more than a big petri dish full of germs. Not his kind of place.

The door opened and a serious looking medical professional walked in with a stethoscope around his neck. "You're awake," he said. "They said you were out."

"Mr. Vandenberg woke just as we pulled up," the paramedic announced.

The doctor walked over, flashed a light in his pupils and felt his head.

"Let's do a CT of his head and C-spine. Also, blood work. Then we'll talk," the doctor told him.

Thirty minutes later, Max promised to rip the next professional who came through that door a new one. The tests were done and still they refused to let Meghan into the room. Until he saw her with his own eyes, he wouldn't believe she hadn't been hurt.

His last memories were of the truck heading towards them on her side of the car. In a last-ditch attempt to avoid the collision, he spun the wheel of the Corvette to swerve in his direction and that was the last thing he remembered.

Throwing back the sheet, he couldn't wait any longer. The paramedics had cut his clothes off and put on one of those ridiculous gowns, but he didn't care. Swinging his legs to the floor, a wave of dizziness swept over him and he sat for a moment letting it pass.

The door to his room swung open. "Mr. Vandenburg, what are you doing? You need to stay in bed."

They had him hooked up to all kinds of wires and monitors,

but he didn't care. He needed to see Meghan.

"No one will let me see my girlfriend and I have to make certain she's all right."

The doctor frowned. "If I allow her in here, will you not get out of bed until all my reports have come back. Then we'll talk."

Max glared at the man in the white coat. "Look, I have a concussion. Playing professional ball, you get two to three a season. Nothing else is wrong with me. I want my girlfriend and I want to go home."

"Let's start with me allowing your girlfriend to come in and we'll go from there," the doctor said. "How would the people of Cupid react if I sent you home and you died tonight? Let me do my job and we'll decide on a treatment plan."

The doctor walked to the door. "What's her name?"

"Meghan," he said, swinging his legs back into bed and covering up with a sheet.

The doctor went outside and when he came back, Meghan stood with him.

"Max, I've been so worried," she said, rushing to his side. Tears rose in her eyes and she let out a shaky breath. "You lay slumped against the window and I kept screaming your name. You didn't answer me. I've never felt so afraid."

He reached up and stroked the side of her face. "Meghan, I'm okay. Got a bit of a headache, but the doctor says he's going to let me go home."

"I don't recall saying that," the man standing in the corner watching them said. "I'm going to check your X rays and we'll make a decision when I return."

The door closed behind him and Meghan all but crawled in bed with him. "No one would tell me anything. All those damn HIPPA laws. It seemed like hours since they brought you in..."

"I'm fine. Worried about you. Everyone kept telling me you're okay, but I had to see you in person. You didn't get hurt?"

"No, I'm all right," she said, leaning over him, her auburn curls spilling around him like a curtain. "Ryan told me you spun the car away from my side. He said you took the brunt of the hit. Did you do that?"

He was unable to admit the truth because then she would gush even more about his protection. At this moment, he was grateful they were both alive. "The last thing I remember is seeing the headlights coming right at us. The cars were on the other side of the highway and I had no place to go. What about the other driver?"

Shaking her head, she said, "Dead and drunk."

An ache welled within him. While he didn't approve of drinking and driving, he never wanted to see someone die from a bad choice. Whoever had been behind the wheel of the truck had lost their life tonight and that left him sad.

"I'm sorry to hear that. But I'm grateful you're alive."

"And I'm grateful you're here where the professionals can help you."

"It's just a concussion and I want to go home."

They'd pulled out of the restaurant parking lot at almost eight o'clock. The clock on the wall showed after ten and he needed some normalcy back in his life.

The door opened and the doctor came in and glanced at Meghan. "Impressive, you managed to keep him in bed."

"Yes," she replied shyly.

The doctor sank down on a stool across from Max. "Good news, the X rays don't show any broken vertebrae or any fractures. We know you have a concussion, but you're used to dealing with those. Your vital signs are all good. As far as I can tell, there is no internal damage, so I'm going to release you. I'd rather you stayed overnight just to make certain everything is all right, but I doubt you're going to agree to stay."

"No," he said, thinking of all the times he spent in the hospital before and how he didn't want to spend another night here.

"That's what I thought. I'll release you if someone will be with you the next twenty-four hours. No sleep for at least another three. Then someone needs to wake you every two hours to make certain you're all right. I'll prescribe some pain pills because tomorrow you're going to feel like a truck ran you over. Over the next couple of days, you are to rest and take it easy. Any problems, any pain, bleeding, anything, come back to the ER."

How many times had he heard this professional spiel?

"All right, Doc, now let me go," he said, knowing he would be dead, dying, or bleeding profusely before he came back to this place.

"Do you have someone you can stay with who can check your pupils every two hours?"

"He can stay at my place," Meghan volunteered. "I'll take care of him."

Max glanced at her. She was going to let him spend the night at her house? Warmth filled him and for the first time that evening since the accident, hope made him smile. Maybe something good would come out of this yet.

"Is that all right?" the doctor asked him.

Hell yes, it was all right. Only one thing could make it be any better. "Yes," he responded while doing a happy dance inside.

"I'll send a nurse in with the discharge papers," he said and walked out the door.

"What does the car look like?" he asked, knowing his beloved Corvette was destroyed. Needing to confirm the awful news. That car was the first thing he bought when he was accepted into the professional football league, his beautiful car.

"You don't want to know. In fact, I'm going to call Uber now to take us home. Ryan brought me to the hospital, but he had to go back to the wreck and help his deputies write the reports."

Picking up her hand, he ran his fingers lightly over the top. "Thanks for letting me stay with you."

"You're welcome. I thought with you being hurt, it was the least I could do. Besides, I'll be safe tonight."

"I'm going to be just fine," he said and brought her hand up to his mouth. Placing his lips on the back of her hand, he kissed it.

If she thought he couldn't have sex because of a concussion, she was dead wrong. In college, when he was hurt worse than this, he'd had sex. Now, he wanted Meghan in the worst possible way. Almost dying did that to a man. Made him remember the important things in life. And being with Meghan was like bringing rays of sunshine into the rain forest.

MEGHAN STAYED by Max's side as she helped him into her home. A nice young man working his way through college had given them a ride to her home. Opening the door, she got him inside and then shut the entryway behind him.

Walking to her couch, he slumped down in the sweatpants the hospital had found for him to wear home. "Would you mind letting me borrow your pink robe? I know whose naked body has been against that cloth. This material, I'm afraid a homeless man wore this before me."

For the first time in hours, laughter bubbled up from within, releasing a rush of emotion. They had survived. "Let me help you into the bathroom and I'll bring it to you."

"Okay," he said. "I'm fine. Occasionally, I get a little dizzy when I move too fast, but other than that, I'm good."

"Still, you need to rest," she said going into her closet and coming back with the pink fluffy covering she'd worn the night of the Cupid dance. That seemed like a long time ago.

"Here," she said, handing him the cover up. "You change and I'll make us some hot cocoa."

When he came out, he handed her the pants and T-shirt. "Burn them, I never want to see them again."

"And you're going home in the nude?"

"No," he said, frowning.

"No car, no pants, no shirt. You're stranded without clothes." Memories of the night he rescued her, left her chest warm with happiness. Now she was helping him, though, her mishap was more lighthearted than a car accident.

A deep sigh escaped him. "Dealing with the insurance company is not going to be fun."

"Don't think about it tonight," she said, bringing him a hot cup of chocolate. Sinking down onto the couch, he scooted beside her.

An overwhelming sense of longing to caress him, make certain he was still alive overcame her. They'd come so close to losing everything.

After she sat the drinks on the coffee table, she turned to him. "Until tonight, all my feelings for you I believed were gone. But seeing you passed out, not even sure you were going to live or die, my heart stopped." A sob escaped, but she managed to get it back under control. "Tomorrow, I don't know what will happen, but this moment, I need to touch you, know you're all right."

Tracing his finger down her cheek, he said softly, "This fluffy piece of covering is not hiding my excitement. I want you so badly."

"You're hurt," she whispered.

"Not bad enough to stop me from being with you," he said, gazing at her in a way that had her insides fluttering like an earthquake.

Reaching up, she pulled his lips down to hers, loving the way his mouth took possession, claiming her. The slide of his hands down to her breasts had her arching against him, wanting, needing him.

Relinquishing her mouth, he stood and held out his hand. "Come on, Meghan. Show me you're feeling the same as I am. A hot scalding need."

"Max," she said with a sigh and took his hand.

How could she deny him when she wanted him as much? When she almost lost him today.

"No one ever made me ache with desire like you do. No one makes me want to fight heaven and earth just to be with you," he said as he walked backward to her bedroom.

A shiver went through her.

"Are you cold? Let me warm you." He pulled her down to the bed.

"I'm not cold. I'm hot for you. I'm shaking because I almost lost you today," she said, her fingertips running down his chest, his stomach, to his manhood. Wrapping her hand around him, he groaned with pleasure. A sense of awe consumed her at his response to her strokes.

"Then let me fix that for you because I want you so much," he said as he gripped her head, holding her mouth hostage. His fingers tangled in her hair, not letting her escape his kiss. And she didn't want to escape. Why with Max did this seem so right, like she found where she belonged? Yet, the scientist in her warned this was her body's reaction to the chemistry between them.

Gently, his fingertips glided down her neck to her shoulders and farther trailing down her chest. Cupping her pale globes, he released her lips and leaned down to lift the soft weight of her breast to his lips.

Tugging on her nipple, he sucked as much of her into his mouth as he could, and she bucked wildly against him, moaning deeply in her throat. Her breathing ragged as her hands moved to his head, trapping him against her breasts as she strained, trying to give him more access to her body.

From the first moment they kissed all those years ago in high school, there had been this craving when they touched. A sensual overload of sensuality connecting them. A simple glance, a caress, a kiss, and a fire ignited, consuming her.

Tenderly, he moved his hand, caressing her skin, skimming her flat stomach, down until he reached her womanly folds.

"Max," she cried, losing herself in the heat of his gaze.

"You feel like silk," he said as he caressed her nether regions.

Slowly, he stroked her as blood pounded in her ears, her heart racing, flooding her senses with desire for Max. As the exhilaration grew inside her, she clutched the sheets. Hot need spiraled through her as her body tightened around his fingers, crying out, shuddering as she stared straight into his soul.

Reaching over to the nightstand, she quickly pulled out a condom, hoping it would hold. The box had sat in her bedroom drawer for over a year, just waiting.

Ripping open the package, she quickly rolled it over him.

"Oh, Meghan," he said as he parted her legs with his. They fit together perfectly. Her breasts touching his chest, her hips supporting him, his manhood nestled between the juncture of her thighs. In a single swift movement, he entered her and she gasped with pleasure.

"Filling me like this is wonderful," she moaned into his ear.

"Meghan."

Staring into his eyes, a connection as strong as an electrical current tethered them as he moved inside, stroking her, loving her. Clutching his back, she clung to him as they rode the waves of passion together, holding onto one another.

A tightening spiral of wanton pleasure filled her, and as much as she wished he could last longer, knew they were both at the crest.

"Max," Meghan called as she writhed beneath his touch.

With a guttural cry, his penis swelled within her, as he slammed into her, convulsing his release. No matter what happened in their future, she would always remember tonight as the night she gave him her heart again.

Chest pounding, their breathing heavy, he rolled them to their sides, pulling her snuggly against his body. Lost in his gaze, he reached down and kissed her on the lips softly, gently for the first time that night.

"Oh, Max, why is it always so good between us," she whispered against him.

EARLY THE NEXT MORNING, Ryan told Taylor about the accident involving Meghan and Max, which completely shocked her. Hurrying over to check on her friend, she imagined the worst. A near head-on collision, she needed to see Meghan was okay.

And ask her what the hell was she thinking going out with Max. The man broke her heart once and it had taken years for her to get over that during her darkest hour, he'd gone off to football camp. Never answering her calls.

The memory of the days and nights of comforting Meghan, helping her recover from Max's deceit were like yesterday. Were they together again?

Standing outside, she rang the doorbell, waiting patiently with coffee and pastries from the restaurant. Saturday, her busiest day at the cafe and she couldn't stay long, but she had to check on her friend and verify Meghan was all right, physically and emotionally.

She pressed the buzzer again, nothing. Could she be passed out in a room somewhere or returned to the hospital?

Taylor knew she kept a hidden spare key. Searching, she quickly found it and put it in the lock. Opening the door, she called out. "Meghan?"

Nothing, no response. Walking through the unit, she saw a strange set of clothing. An man's ugly warm-up suit. That was odd. Continuing on, she yelled again, "Meghan? Are you here?"

A moan sounded from the area of the bedroom and she walked a little faster. Was she lying on the floor hurt? Rushing into Meghan's room, a rumpled bed greeted her. "Meghan?"

The sound of water running sent her hurrying toward the bathroom. Yanking open the door, the vision she witnessed would be burned on her brain forever.

Max had Meghan up against the shower wall, and oh my God, they were soaping each other. "Meghan!"

"Aargh, Taylor, what are you doing here. Get out."

"Get dressed and meet me in the living room," she said. Furious that the man who broke her friend's heart was up to no good, she pointed at Max. "And you, too."

All but running out the door, she couldn't believe what she'd seen. Thank goodness, she hadn't seen any body parts as the frosted door design hid the bodies from view.

After she walked into the kitchen, she poured coffee into cups, needing a moment to compose herself before she faced Meghan. What was the girl thinking? But then again, isn't that what Kelsey said about Ryan?

A few minutes later, Meghan appeared in the doorway, wearing yoga pants and a T-shirt.

"Why are you here?"

"Because I was worried about you. Ryan told me this morning you were involved in a serious car crash in Max's Corvette. I'm glad you're safe, but I'm shocked. Don't forget how upset you were when he refused to take your phone calls, when you thought you were pregnant."

Sinking down on a chair, Meghan stared at Taylor, her face pink from the shower and her other activities. "You're right. Last night he lost consciousness and they wouldn't let him stay alone, so he came back to my place."

"The two of you just jumped in the sack together."

"Kind of."

"Are you willing to take the chance of getting hurt a second time? Are you on birth control pills?"

"No. We used a condom last night."

Shaking her head, Taylor raised her brows at her friend. "What about this morning?"

"Uh, you interrupted us," she said, glancing back toward Max as if he waited for her to return. "He doesn't have any clothes here. The hospital cut them off him, so he can't leave. Plus, he doesn't have any transportation. His car is demolished."

Taylor laughed. "That's fitting."

"At the accident, I feared he was dead. It scared me. Both of us could have been seriously injured or even killed. I thought I'd lost him for good."

"Are you in love with him again?" Taylor asked, trying to read her friends beautiful face.

"I don't know," Meghan said sheepishly and Taylor didn't believe her. The past had caught up with them. M&M were back together.

The handwriting was on the wall, even if Meghan didn't want to admit her love. Not wanting to see her friend suffer again, Taylor tried not to be negative.

Sure, they had been young, but leaving your girlfriend to deal with a possible teenage pregnancy and never calling her while you're gone, was cold. Meghan deserved better.

"Look, it's none of my business, but remember what happened before. Remember how he deserted you. Why would you let him do that to you again? Especially now that you're studying to become Dr. Scott. You don't need him to take you off course. Think of your dreams and desires."

Meghan picked up her coffee cup and walked to the window in the kitchen looking out. "Everything you're saying I hear and I lived through his deceit. He hurt me badly. There is so much chemistry between us. The desire is just like seven years ago, before he left."

Taylor looked at her watch. This was not hers to decide. It was Megan's choice. "It's your life. If you want to take the risk, it's your decision."

Glancing back at her, Meghan sighed. "I'll send him away as soon as I'm certain he's all right."

Standing, Taylor walked over and gave Meghan a hug. "I've got to run. We didn't talk about the wreck. Are you okay?"

Nodding, she gulped. "I'm fine. Scared ten years off my life, but at least I'm still walking. The other guy didn't make it."

"Ryan told me. The thought of losing my friend, frightened me senseless," she said.

"Then you came over to find me and Max together," Meghan said with a laugh. "Maybe the car accident damaged me more than I thought. It certainly left my heart open for a freeway crash."

CHAPTER 8

$\mathcal{M}$ ax couldn't find anything to wear besides Meghan's pink fluffy robe. Appearing ridiculous while storming out to tell Taylor to mind her own business was not his strong suit. What happened between him and Meghan was no one's concern. By the time the cover up no longer had a tent in the front, Taylor had left.

And frankly, last night had been the best night of sex he ever experienced. As a pro ball player, women threw themselves at him, offering him anything he wanted. Looking back, he wasn't proud of the fact he partook what football bunnies offered.

Young, with temptation flaunted at him, it took maturing to realize that wasn't the kind of woman he wanted as his wife.

What he wanted was the relationship he and Meghan once had. One of love and happiness and happily ever after. Once she explained to him what made her choose to abort their baby did they have a chance?

All he required was for the two of them to sit down and her to tell him why she decided to end her pregnancy that fateful summer. Why couldn't she wait for him to return and the two of them decide what they could offer their child.

More than anything, he longed to put the past behind him, but first he needed to learn why. They'd talked about wanting children, once they each fulfilled their dreams. Then they would start their family. After the abortion, she texted him to tell him they were done, leaving him destitute.

Just thinking about it all over again, he felt himself tensing. The air needed clearing before they could go any further.

Wrapping the pink robe around him, he strolled into the living room. Meghan stood in the center with a cup of coffee, staring off into space.

"Did she leave?"

"Yes, she was concerned about me when Ryan told her about the crash."

"Does everyone in town know where you keep your blasted key?"

A frown crossed her beautiful face. "No. Only a few friends and my family."

"So every time we have sex at your place, should I bring in the key?"

With a shrug, her emerald eyes flashed with annoyance. "I see no problem with the key."

Why did he sense hostility radiating from her when moments earlier, she'd been a sweet, pliant lover?

"Yes, it's an issue for me when people walk in while we're having sex. Being interrupted, threatened, and told to get my clothes on by your psycho friends during our most private, sacred, time pisses me off."

The moment the words left his mouth, he regretted them. Taylor wasn't a psycho, just very protective of Meghan and he respected she watched out for her friend, but not that she stormed in demanding he get out.

"Taylor reminded me, I let the present overcome the past. I've forgotten how you went away that weekend, thinking I was pregnant, never calling me. Never checking on me. Never responding to my texts."

"Hey, I was a young teenage boy on his way to college. Going on a football scholarship I knew for the next four years the university owned me. If they told me to jump, I asked how high. If they told me to run, I sprinted.

"When I walked into that first training camp, they took our cell phones away. What you don't know is I couldn't call you until Sunday, on my way home. By that time, you'd gone away to school. You ran out on me. You wouldn't even return my phone calls."

That hurt more than anything. Why did she try to make it appear he was at fault? She never gave them the chance to talk about what happened. To this day, she still had never admitted to him she aborted their baby.

The elephant in the room separated them and he longed to expose the monster, but could see he was barely treading water. Anger radiated from her body and he realized she still declined to discuss their past. While he wanted to sit down and talk rationally and civilly, she denied their problems.

"Please, leave. An Uber driver should be here any moment. Here are your sweatpants the hospital gave you to wear home."

Anger gripped his stomach like a machine vise. Why wouldn't she try?

"Why is it every time I think we have a chance, you prove to me we don't. Are you afraid of the past because you might be wrong? Instead, your friend comes rushing over and reminds you of the wrong I supposedly did to you. I'm tired of trying to reason with you."

Grabbing the clothes, he'd sworn never to put on again, he walked into the bathroom where he slammed the door. His body ached, but his chest throbbed with frustration. Maybe he couldn't fix a broken relationship with the promise of a life together. Maybe the time to let go had come. He was done.

&

THE DOOR SLAMMED and Max walked out of her life, probably forever. A deep crushing hurt filled her and she sank down on the couch and cried. During the last few weeks, the spark they had from high school had been rekindled.

Spending time with Max, she enjoyed his company, he did things for her that made her feel less geeky and instead pretty. Yet, somehow this morning it all came crashing down.

Last night, witnessing him injured frightened her and left her questioning everything. How would she cope if Max had died? Her blood went cold at the thought of never seeing him again. No matter what, she wanted him to be happy and healthy and alive.

Before Taylor arrived, she meant to tell him they should talk about the past. Just once. Taylor's visit reminded her of the nights spent crying over Max. The depression following her break-up with him. The way she ran away to college to escape the heartbreak.

After the things Max confessed, what if she'd been wrong?

What if it was true, he couldn't call her, then she would be at fault. Did she overreact when he never called? She felt like this was how college would be. He would have his friends, including a new girlfriend and she would be left behind. Everything would be more important than the girl he left in Cupid.

So, she released him and hoped he did well. Giving up Max had been hard. Even now, she still loved him, still needed him. How could he be the first and only man she loved.

Sure, there were others, but no one claimed her heart like Max. No one she wanted to tie the knot with. No one she pictured a home and kids with. No one she wanted to spend eternity with.

When he left, he'd been furious. She didn't think she would

hear from him again. And while part of her wanted to, the other part told her that was a wise decision.

But if breaking up was for the best, why did it feel so wrong. Like she had made the biggest mistake of her life.

MEGHAN GLANCED AROUND at her friends as they sat in their bathrobes with their hair up in towels, drinking a glass of wine, receiving a pedicure. They'd already gotten a massage and a facial. So far the day had been fun.

Tonight, they planned to dine at an expensive restaurant and were staying at an exclusive hotel in downtown Dallas.

Meghan laid back in the chair with her eyes closed. "This is the life. We should plan on doing this at least once a quarter."

After the last week, the break-up with Max and the wreck, she needed some relaxation. Some down time where her brain concentrated on something other than the pain she felt. Why didn't Max fight for her? If they were so good together, why didn't he fight to keep her? Why didn't she fight to keep Max?

Confusion racked her mind, her soul, even her body seemed out of kilter. Could she be having a delayed reaction to the accident? But she would never let Max know.

"Maybe," Kelsey said, watching the young man wrap her legs in a towel. "Depends on how the shop does."

"If I can find someone to cover the diner, I'm game," Taylor said.

Kelsey sighed. "I have a confession to make."

Why did her voice hold an ominous tone? What would Kelsey share?

"Ryan came to see me yesterday. After almost seven years, we finally put to bed the past. He apologized about how he hurt me."

"What?" Meghan said. "I knew you guys broke up, but what did he do."

"He cheated," Taylor said. "An apology doesn't make it right."

"He had some excellent points. He admitted to being a young, horny boy who just wanted to get into any girl's pants. And when you add tequila and a willing teenage girl to a high school party, you get trouble."

Oh God, why was it that men deemed they deserved a hall pass for what they did in school. Then again, she made some of the worst decisions at that time in her life. Some she was still reeling from. Some she didn't know if she did the right thing or not. She would probably never know regarding Max.

"Still, doesn't excuse what he did," Taylor said.

"Hmm," Meghan replied. "Did you ever have too much to drink in college and do something stupid?"

Maybe Ryan was just like the rest of them and made a bad mistake. A good guy who lived and learned like all of them. The night of the wreck, Ryan stayed by her side until he was certain Max was going to live. Then he left to return to the scene of the accident.

"I certainly did. It was a wonder I graduated," Taylor said.

"I told you how I popped my cherry. No, I'm not proud. What makes me any different from Ryan?" Kelsey asked.

"Did he do this to convince you to talk me into going out with him again?" Taylor asked.

Kelsey laughed. "No, we didn't discuss you much. Though for only being on one date, the man seemed pretty crazy about you. You kept us in the dark regarding you and Ryan."

Meghan sat up, her eyes widening with surprise. "You and Ryan? Seeing one another? Really?"

She started laughing and sunk back on the chair. She'd been suspicious when she had root beer floats with Taylor but she denied dating the sheriff.

No, it couldn't be. It just couldn't.

The scientist in her didn't want to believe that dancing around the Cupid statue brought them love. Taylor was dating

Ryan and she and Max had come together again. Or at least until this week tore them apart. Who was Kelsey secretly meeting on the sly?

"Yes, me and Ryan," Taylor said. "But he lied to me."

"What person hasn't told a fib to make themselves look better," Kelsey said. "You've never distorted or misrepresented something? Never kept anything from your friends?"

"Okay, so I didn't tell you the truth about Ryan."

Meghan snickered softly. They weren't thinking about the Cupid dance. They hadn't considered how they put themselves on the line to find happily ever after believing in a silly superstition. Taylor had found love and Meghan had found love, who was trying to capture Kelsey's heart?

"Do you love him?" Kelsey asked.

Meghan and Kelsey stared at their friend. Clearly, she cared about Ryan, but would she confess to love? Did she realize that Cupid Stupid dance worked its magic on her and Ryan?

"Yes, I love Ryan," she said almost shouting the words.

Kelsey smiled. "Good."

"Are you happy now?" Taylor asked.

Neither of her friends had caught on that the Cupid Stupid dance was working. All were on their way to love and pleasure, except Meghan, who managed to screw it up, yet, again. When would she learn?

For a smart woman, she had a difficult time with relationships.

"Why are you letting an incident that happened almost seven years ago stop you from getting the love you deserve? Why would you let the mistakes between us keep you from happiness?" Kelsey said, her voice rising with disbelief.

"He had sex with someone else while the two of you dated," Taylor said vehemently. "I vowed never to date another man who can't be faithful. Ryan wasn't loyal."

Kelsey smiled that knowing grin. "At eighteen, he wanted to

lose his virginity. I wanted to surrender mine in college. Now, if he did that today, then yes, I'd be getting a rope and we'd be stringing him up in the Cupid courtyard in the town square. He wasn't the only one who screwed up. You hid this relationship from us."

"Only to protect you. You've said how much you dislike him," Taylor said.

"And I did. Yesterday, we buried the hatchet. Life is too short and he said he was sorry. How many men apologize and admit their error," Kelsey said, gazing at her friend. Picking up Taylor's hand, she shook her head. "You admitted you love him. Give him a break. Give him some time."

Oh my God. Kelsey was forgiving Ryan and Taylor had fallen in love with him. The Cupid statue was working overtime, while she managed to ricochet his arrow by loving and losing once again.

Busting out laughing, she stared at her friends unable to contain the hysterical giggle erupting from her even louder.

"All right, I'll give him another opportunity, but I'm going to lay down some rules. This will only happen on my terms."

"Great," Kelsey said and jumped out of the foot spa much to the technician's dismay. Splashing water all over the floor in her exuberance to reach out and embrace Taylor. Meghan bounced up, giggling, tracking water everywhere and joined in the group hug.

The giggles spilled from her, sounding almost hysterical.

"Why have you laughed this entire time?" Taylor demanded to know.

"Don't you see," Meghan said smiling. "The Cupid superstition is finding us love. You're the first one to succumb to the spell."

Taylor would find her happily ever after, while Meghan once again, had to heal her broken heart. Once you love someone, body and soul, was it possible to love anyone else? Could she be in love forever with Max while he hated her.

CHAPTER 9

*M*eghan kept thinking that soon she would accept she and Max were now in the past. But every day she felt tired, depressed, and a little anxious.

Why couldn't she just move on? The last month she concentrated on the end of the school year and her final classes. Hopefully, before long, this virus would release her and she would return to feeling like her old self again. Not breaking down crying at the least little thing.

As she walked into the teacher's lounge, she froze. Max sat beside flirty, Christy Selleck talking about English prep. Really? Christy? Couldn't he find someone who had more of a brain?

Refusing to let him know he was getting to her, she strolled over and placed her lunch on the table. At the stench of tuna, her stomach roiled, the warning leaving her nauseous. The fishy odor overpowered her and she could feel herself gagging.

This was the second time this week the smell of someone's midday meal had overcome her, sending her racing out in search of clean air. Last time she picked up her stuff and left. This time, she needed to sit down for a few minutes.

The room spun eerily as she sank down into the chair, she

glanced around. They were the only three in the lounge.

"It's been such a pleasure talking to you," Christy said, leaning down and giving him an eyeful of her breasts. "This is my lunch period. Maybe I'll see you here again tomorrow."

"I'll see what I can work out," he said not committing, but leaving it open. Why did Meghan care? He was free to date anyone he pleased.

Suddenly the tuna accosted her nose, causing her to gag. Rising from the chair, she all but ran into the bathroom. Unable to stop herself, the contents of her stomach erupted like a geyser. Oh great, just great. The sounds of her upchucking echoed in the small space and she realized everyone in the teacher's lounge could hear her. Including Max.

Standing, she leaned against the wall for a few minutes before she washed her hands and wiped her mouth.

When she finally opened the door, he stood there looking like a million dollars, staring at her.

"Are you okay?" he asked, gazing at her. "You got over the wreck, right? Don't want you to claim the accident caused you to become ill."

Irritation gripped her as she walked past him. Not only was she dealing with a stupid stomach bug, but now she had to deal with Max as well.

"You're fine. I won't hold you responsible. Just a touch of a virus."

Sinking down at the table, she wanted to lay her head down and rest. Though, she went to bed earlier, the virus drained her energy. This flu bug was quite the doozy, draining her of stamina, sapping her strength, making her emotional.

Frowning, he stared at her, shooting daggers at her with his eyes. "You don't look too good. You're pale."

"Usually that happens when you're sick," she said, wishing his attention was anywhere besides her. Yet she also had the most incredible urge to sit in his lap and have a soul wrenching cry.

About that time her stomach rebelled again. Jumping up, she ran to the ladies' room, barely making it in time. This time the dry heaves were upon her and she knew she would not be eating anything for a while.

Walking out of the restroom, he waited. "Why don't you go home and get some rest. Otherwise, this is going to spread through the school affecting a lot of people. Let me drive you home."

Shaking her head, she didn't want to be alone with him. Even being sick in his company, she'd be tempted.

"Thank you, but my car is here," she said.

"Good, we'll take yours and then I'll bring it back later tonight."

"How do I know you won't rob a bank or something in my car?"

Laughing he shook his head. "Even when you're sick, you're still a smart-ass."

"Hey, maybe I have a reason to be one."

Growing weaker by the moment, she didn't want him to take her home, but she was about to collapse. Her biggest fear was that someone would come into the teacher's lounge to heat their lunch. The scent of cooking food would send her racing into the bathroom bowing down to the porcelain god, begging for him to make it stop.

"All right, you can take me home. Let me tell Principal--"

Unable to wait, she took off running to the toilet again. What if she couldn't make it home without vomiting out the window or something equally gross.

Five minutes later, she walked into the lounge. He stood waiting with her purse, her keys, and her lunch all neatly wrapped up.

"I've told the principal. Another teacher is going to watch the library and I'm driving you home."

There was no strength left to argue.

"Let's go."

Taking her stuff from him, together they walked out the door.

All the way home, she sat quietly, hoping she could make it home without throwing up in her car. And without a confrontation. No longer did she have the willpower to fight him. They pulled up in front of her condo and he came around to open her door.

"Thank you for bringing me home," she said. Glancing up at him, it dawned on her. "For a man who ran out on me in the past, lately you're always coming to my rescue."

His body bristled and she knew it was the wrong thing to say. Over and over, he'd rescued her. First with the Cupid dance, then her car battery, the science teacher, the accident and now bringing her home when she fell ill.

The virus must be eating her brain for her say things that were so stupid and badly timed.

"I'm sorry that sounded ungrateful. Please understand, I appreciate that you always seem to help me."

"What the hell are you talking about? I didn't run out on you. You left me. You went to school early to avoid me."

Part of what he said was true. Right now, she couldn't deal with this. Her vision was blurring and she would either faint or throw up and she didn't know which would happen first.

"Please, I can't talk about this now."

"That's the problem. You never want to explain the past. There is always an excuse. No matter what I do, I'm always in the wrong. Name a time and a date. We're going to talk about this and move on."

She held up her hand. "All right. Let me get to the point I can drink water. Then we'll talk."

Needing to escape, not only the angry vibrations between them, but also the sense of longing, she hurried up the steps to her door, leaving him behind.

Today, she was in no shape to consider discussing what had

happened in the past. But soon, she would face him.

❦

DAMN IT! Why did watching Meghan so sick frighten him? Seeing her ill made him long to look after her.

How did a husband cope with the sight of his wife being sick? Observing Meghan, so pale and white, worried him. No matter what happened between them, she seemed to always be the woman he wanted more than anyone.

In the last month, he forced himself to date, trying to eject her from his mind and mend his heart, but no one compared. No one he wanted to go out with a second time.

Now Christy Selleck was hitting on him big time at school. Flashing her breasts at him, bumping into him in the halls and it was all he could do to keep from running the other direction.

The teacher was a beautiful woman, but he still wanted Meghan.

Since his return to Cupid, he thought they might have another chance. Then Taylor came over interrupting them. From that moment, things had gone to hell in a hand basket. What she said to Meghan, he had no idea, but she ran faster than the track team.

Tearing him up inside, leaving his chest ripped apart. He loved Meghan. Had loved and wanted to marry her for more years than he cared to remember. Thoughts of the two of them together flowed through him like a gentle river, reminding him of all the good times.

The night he picked her up stark naked in the middle of the street, he thought might be a new beginning for them.

She was his one. One and only. And he wanted to love her until he took his last breath.

After Taylor left, rage filled him that Meghan abstained from being with him. What about the past kept her from accepting his love? How could he care about her so much when she didn't fight for them? Maybe he needed to move on.

Instead, the last five weeks he spent raging against the insurance company and missing Meghan even worse than when he left for college.

He needed to recognize she didn't want him and let her go, but part of him refused to give up.

At least this time, he didn't dream of what their child looked like. He wasn't mourning the loss of a baby. At least this time she wasn't...

Like a slap to the face, it hit him. Slamming on the brakes of her car, he pulled over to the side of the road. In his mind, he did the calculations.

Five weeks ago, they had sex. At first, they used a condom, but when they were in the shower...nothing came between them.

"Damn," he said and punched the gas.

Like a circular wheel, they were right back where they started. But by golly, this time, if she was expecting, things would be a lot different. This time she wouldn't...he couldn't think the word or say it.

If she was having his baby, this time his child would be wanted. The old clunker's tires spun out as he headed toward the nearest store to purchase a pregnancy test.

LESS THAN AN HOUR LATER, Meghan was lying in bed, trying to doze off when the front door opened.

"Meghan, where are you?"

The nausea was better and she'd stopped throwing up, but she still felt weak and tired.

Just because Max knew where the key was didn't mean he was supposed to use it to come and go when he pleased. Slowly rising from bed, she walked into the living area.

SYLVIA MCDANIEL

"Why did you come back? I'm changing the locks," she said doubting she would, but wanting him to think she meant it.

"This time around, we're doing it my way. If you're pregnant, you're not getting rid of my child."

Shock rippled through her and she felt confused.

"Are you high? What the hell are you talking about? I never aborted your baby. In fact, I..."

Sudden dawning rushed to her face.

His eyes widened and he took a step back, confused. "Right before I left for football camp in Austin, you told me you thought you might be expecting. Just as soon as I could, I drove back to Cupid to learn you'd broken up with me, gone to college, and aborted my baby. If I'd been in town, I would have stopped you, but you made your decision, never thinking to include me, the father."

"I texted. I called. I did everything possible to contact you, but you never responded."

Max clenched his fists, then slowly opened them. "Remember, they took our phones while I was in football camp. No outside interference. Later, I tried to call you; I got nothing."

"I blocked your calls."

"Did you lose the baby?"

Of all the asinine things to assume, she wanted to punch him. She never had been expecting. Never. "No, I texted and I called you. No response. The doctor assured me it was a false alarm."

The color drained from his face and he turned white. Sinking down into a chair, he rubbed his hands over his face. "All these years, I believed you aborted our child."

An ache centered in her chest. "That would never happen."

All the fears of that time returned, and she glared at him.

"Since you didn't respond, I assumed you didn't want to speak to me. I thought you didn't want to tell me you weren't ready for babies. I thought I would be a single parent taking care of our son or daughter alone.

"The doctor examined me and told me due to the stress of graduation and preparing to leave for school, my body was reacting. The test had to be old and showed a false positive.

"Max, I've never been more afraid. Too young to raise a child, unable to end a life if I was pregnant. I didn't know what to do. And you were nowhere to be found."

The tone had gone from raised voices, to soft tinged with sadness. Meghan sighed. She should have talked to him. He deserved to know the truth. Yes, he'd been excluded, though she tried to reach him to tell him there was no pregnancy. For a moment, she imagined how she would feel if he didn't include her and she realized he had a right to be angry.

"All this time, I thought the worst and couldn't understand why you didn't include me," he said, sighing.

Walking to his side, she sank down beside him. "Is this what you wanted to talk about for months?"

"Yes, and you wouldn't. You kept saying I left you."

"That's because I thought you had. Leaving, you acted like I was keeping you from your dreams. I felt like a burden. The doctor said there was no baby. That news was such a relief - yet I was disappointed you reacted the way you did. And still no word from you. I couldn't share the fear or the happiness with you. You had disappeared."

Taylor had kept her from losing her mind until she left for school early, wanting to get away before Max returned.

With a sigh, he shook his head. "All my life I wanted to be a football player. A couple of days before I leave for the biggest football camp of my scholarship, you tell me you're late. I was scared. I loved you - but I wanted a chance to fulfill my dream and a baby would make that damn near impossible.

"On the way home, I made the decision we would get married and have the child regardless if I played ball. And then you were gone."

For the first time, a moment of silence filled the room as they sat absorbing the consequences of two kids not ready for the real world.

"From my text, I thought you understood."

"Your text said, 'Pregnancy problem resolved. Obviously, you've moved on. I'm moving on. Have a great life.'"

"Oh," she said, her mouth frowning. "That's not very clear."

"Hell no, it's not. I though you got rid of our child. Especially since you refused to discuss the past."

A deep sense of sorrow consumed Meghan for everything they lost. Not clearly explaining what happened wounded him deeply. Tears welled up in her eyes. That time right before leaving Cupid had been stressful.

"I'm sorry. My imagination went crazy when you didn't call, thinking you wanted to end it with me, so you could attend college. Once I knew there was no baby, I was angry and I cut you off. If we had communicated, this would be behind us. But I was so furious, you hadn't called - when I needed you the most you weren't there."

Running his hand through his hair, he turned to look at her. "You're not the only one who was wrong. We both made mistakes. You're right. Somehow I should have gotten a message to you that I had no phone."

The illness, the tension, left her feeling worn out. But what brought him back to her house so quickly? He came running in here determined and saying this time things were going to be different. "What made you come back just now?"

With a sigh, he glanced at her. "On the way back to school, I thought, oh my God, what if she's pregnant again."

Meghan gasped and drew back, her mind quickly rewinding to the date of her last period. Oh no, not again, not again, this couldn't happen again.

"No," she said. "We used protection."

He grimaced. "Except when we were in the shower. Remember, we got a little frisky that morning, before Taylor showed up.

Five minutes earlier, she would have witnessed us doing more than just soaping each other down."

How could she be so stupid? So reckless.

Getting up, he walked over to her counter where a sack sat and held it. "All those thoughts caused the past to resurface... When I came through the door, I said this time is going to be different and I meant it."

As he reached into the plastic bag, he pulled out a new pregnancy test. Her heart beat faster as she stared at the box in his hands, biting her lips. She wasn't afraid, but nervous. Very nervous.

Taking her hand, he gazed at her, his eyes serious. "For the first time in many years, we both recognize what went wrong in our past. While I'm relieved there was never a baby, we also mishandled the situation and caused a lot of painful feelings between us."

Gripping her hand, he squeezed it hard and gazed into her eyes. "This month has been miserable for me. The time we spend together, the dates, even the wreck drew us closer and made me happy. You make me a smarter person, I laugh more with you, I want more time with you. I have always loved you. Life is better with you by my side. Meghan, you are the woman I want to wake up beside each morning and fall asleep with at night for the rest of my life."

She started to cry, tears rolling down her face at his words. In the last month, she had existed but felt like a piece of herself was missing.

Placing the box on the counter, he turned back to her. "Regardless of this test, I love you." In the middle of her living room, he dropped to one knee. "This comes from my heart, even though not the most romantic proposal. But one I can't put off any longer. Whether or not you're expecting our child, I want to make you mine. Would you please do me the honor of being my wife."

With a gasp, she lunged herself at him, knocking him to the floor where he cradled her on top of him, taking the brunt of the fall. "Fighting is not what I want to do with you. I want a family, to grow old together and love you until the day I leave this earth. I love you, Max. Yes, I'll marry you."

Her mouth covered his in a kiss that held all the longing she'd been holding back just for him. Their lips finally came apart and he stared into her eyes. "From here on out, we're going to make certain we each understand. All major decisions are made in sync. We are a team."

"Whatever your dreams, let's talk about them together. I want you to be happy," she said.

"I want you to be happy," he echoed.

They lay there for a few more minutes holding one another. Yet, her curiosity was tormenting her. She had to know.

"Are you ready?" she asked.

"What, to see if you're pregnant?"

"We'll make an appointment with the doctor to get the results confirmed and move forward from there."

"This time, we won't let this come between us," he said, gazing at her.

"If I'm pregnant, we created this life together," she said, squeezing his hand, ready to face this possibility.

"Agreed. What are the odds?"

Sitting up, she frowned for a moment and did the calculations in her head. "There is a forty percent chance I'm expecting. We made love during the highest ovulation period, so if your guys were strong enough to swim upstream, we could be having a child."

Jumping to his feet, he reached down and held out his hand grinning. "Let's find out if we're having a baby."

A thrill went through her and she suddenly wanted to have his child more than anything.

CHAPTER 10

*M*eghan stared around the table at her girlfriends. Taylor had recently gotten engaged to Ryan, and Kelsey...she didn't know what was up with that girl, but her face glowed and she seemed to have a sparkle about her that had been missing.

"Why aren't you drinking?" Taylor asked, staring at her in a quizzical manner. "You're always sipping on a glass of wine."

"No alcohol for me right now," she said. "Besides, I called this meeting to share some news."

"Oh?" Kelsey said. "Last time we got together, Taylor told us about Ryan's proposal. What kind of news do you have?"

"I'm pregnant," she said smiling. She still couldn't believe it. It didn't seem real and yet she was so happy and poor Max was busting at the seams. They'd told their parents last night and the wedding plans were already in full swing.

"Oh my God, that son of a bitch, I'll kill him for hurting you again," Taylor said. "I don't care if he is some big football star. He is not getting away with this."

Meghan started laughing and put her hand on Taylor's arm. "It's okay. Everything is resolved and we're back together."

"What?" Kelsey demanded. "When did this happen."

"The night we danced around the Cupid statue," she said with a laugh. "In three weeks, we're getting married and I want you girls to stand up with me."

Meghan still suffered from morning sickness and the doctor warned her that would last for a couple months, but she and Max had been so excited when they left the doctor's office with the news.

This time the pregnancy was real. This time they were having a baby and they couldn't wait to see their little peanut.

"Are you certain this time?" Taylor asked.

Meghan laughed. "We're already designing the nursery. And he bought a family car. No more Corvettes. He's telling me he wants his own football team, and I'm saying, let's just work on the first one before we start talking about the next baby."

Kelsey jumped up and hugged her. "I'm so happy for you."

"As long as he's going to be a good husband and father, I'm happy as well," Taylor said. Her eyes widened. "Oh my goodness, I bet it happened when I walked in on you guys in the shower."

Meghan grinned. "Well, the conception probably occurred five minutes before, but we were finished when you showed up."

"That makes me his or her official godmother."

Kelsey stared between the two of them and Meghan quickly filled her in on what happened.

"You know, I didn't believe in this Cupid superstition. But I'm engaged, Meghan is expecting a baby and about to be married. Kelsey you're next."

She smiled. "Don't worry about me. I've got a cowboy by the tail."

Cupid's Dance - Kelsey's Story

CODY GRAHAM SANG to the country ballad on the radio in his truck, trying to stay awake, knowing he was almost home. He'd spent the day at a livestock auction in West Texas and was returning a little poorer, exhausted, but pleased with his purchases. The ranch needed some new bloodlines and he'd found exactly what he'd been looking for.

The new heifers would be delivered next week. Afterward, he'd gone to dinner with some buddies and now the four-hour trip was almost behind him. He could collapse in his own bed and wake up refreshed and ready to clean the barns tomorrow.

A flicker of light reflected off something ahead and he shook his head to clear his eyes staring at what appeared to be a woman hiding behind a tree.

His headlights flashed and he did a double take. Knowing she'd been seen, the naked woman was running down the street her arm stretched across her breast, her hand in front of her vagina. He pulled up beside her and slowed, not certain how to handle this situation, not wanting to frighten her, but thinking something terrible must have happened.

Rolling down the window, he called, "Ma'am, are you in some kind of trouble?"

Kelsey Lawrence turned and glared at him, her eyes widening with recognition and fright.

He hit the brake and put the truck in park. Yanking open the truck door, he strode around the back of the truck to her. Damn, she was a good-looking woman with all those curves and soft, tempting skin just beckoning him. But he remembered the promise he'd made to her brothers, his best friends back in high school.

Stay away from our sister. She's off limits.

If she was hurt, he'd help her brothers find and injure the guy who did this to her.

All of their friends were held to the same code. Kelsey was off limits. Yet, here she was naked as the day she was born, her womanly curves, a mouthwatering temptation to even this tired cowboy.

"Cody," she said, stopping.

He slipped off his coat and wrapped it around her. "Get in the truck. Then you can tell me what happened."

He didn't offer her an option. Her brothers were going to have a fit and while he didn't know what sent her fleeing down the street naked, there would be hell to pay somewhere.

"Are you certain?" she asked.

"Get in the truck before you freeze to death," he said. "Then we can talk."

Opening the truck door, he stood beside it waiting for her to crawl in, wanting to help her, but uncertain as to where to put his hands without appearing a pervert.

She glanced back behind her and then crawled inside.

Cody stalked around to the driver's door and climbed in. When he got inside, he turned up the heater in the cab.

"Oh goodness, I don't think I will ever take heat for granted again."

"What happened? Do I need to call the police?"

Shaking her head, she gazed at him, her big brown eyes pleading. "Please don't. We were dancing naked around the Cupid statue when they showed up."

Stunned, he stared at her, all the fright he'd kept at bay changed to laughter. A warm feeling spread throughout his chest. He wanted to throw back his head and laugh out loud, yet he remembered Kyle and Drew telling him they had just moved Kelsey back to Cupid. But still, who believed that Cupid nonsense?

Managing to keep the laugh inside, he grinned at her. "You that desperate for love? I'd think a fine woman like you would be beating them off with a stick."

Available At All Retailers!

Thank You For Reading!

Dear Reader,

Thanks for reading! When I was trying to decide what book to write for a Valentine's box set, I remembered that years ago, I wrote a story set in Cupid, Texas. I decided to go back to that little town and bring in new characters. I hope you enjoy the Cupid superstition. And yes, there are more stories about Cupid coming.

As always, if you're inclined, I would appreciate you letting everyone know by posting your comments on your favorite retailer. Whether or not you loved the book or hated, it-I'd enjoy your feedback.

Join my Facebook readers group, where we talk books, stories and mainly have a good time. Click here and tell us why you read romance.

Sign up for my new book alerts if you'd like to learn about my releases before everyone else. Thanks for venturing into my world and I hope to see you here again soon.

Yours in Drama, Divas, Bad Boys and Romance!
Sincerely,

Sylvia McDaniel

www.SylviaMcDaniel.com
Sylvia@SylviaMcDaniel.com

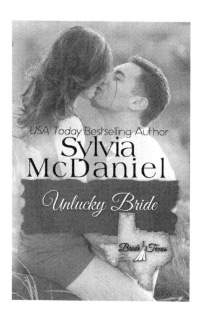

USA Today Bestselling Author
Sylvia
McDaniel
Unlucky Bride
Bride, Texas

Chapter One

Cupid, Texas

"Laney Baxter, if you have reservations, back out now," Ally, her best friend and bridesmaid said. "Your son doesn't need a father that badly."

Reaching up, Laney touched the gold heart necklace around her neck. Maybe not, but the boy was growing from toddler to little boy, and her son would do better with the influence of a strong man.

Deliberately, she kept her son's father's identity a secret. No one needed to know, not her family, her friends, or even her best friend. For one thing, it would lead to all kinds of questions she was too embarrassed to explain. Especially to her parents.

"Not really reservations. Roger is just not who I envisioned marrying," Laney admitted, not willing to concede she dreamed of walking down the aisle with Ally's brother Chase.

"Do you love him? Please tell me you are not shackling yourself to a man you don't care about."

"Of course, I love Roger. He's a good man. But I expected I would be more excited about tomorrow," she confessed.

Roger was everything she could want. Patient and kind, he agreed to wait to consummate their relationship. After the pee stick changed color, she made the decision that until a ring graced her left finger and a license proclaimed her his wife, there would be no sharing her bed. What was that old saying?

Once burned, twice shy.

"Don't you think your lack of excitement is telling?"

Flipping her shoulder length brown hair back, she shook her head. "After being heartbroken by Trenton's dad, the disappearance of Jim, nothing about love excites me anymore. My lack of excitement is my attempt to guard my heart."

After an unplanned pregnancy and an abandoned engagement, when it came to men, caution was best.

Ally tossed back her glass of wine. "In high school, you were always the life of the party. Creating more mischief than any of the other girls we hung with. And yet, here you are the night before your big day holed up with me in The Cupid Love Nest bed and breakfast. Not even a bachelorette night on the town. We should be down at Valentino's bar drinking champagne and being toasted."

With a shrug, she said, "I'm a parent now. My son is my first priority."

The idea of getting drunk wasn't appealing. She only planned on marrying once and a clear head was optimal when she took her vows. What if Trenton became sick or called for her? He didn't need an out of control mother.

"Lord, I never realized how much having a child could change a person."

A laugh came from Laney's lips as she considered how her life had changed since Trenton arrived. At first, she'd been distraught over having a child. Now, Trenton was a blessing. When he grinned and held up his arms, her heart clenched with love for her little man. Forsaking her single lifestyle was easy.

Her only regret was his father.

Barely three years of age, Trenton's birth transformed her world for the better.

"Your mom is keeping him while you two go off on your honeymoon?"

"No honeymoon. We're spending the night in Fort Worth, and Sunday, we'll come back here. Monday, I move into his apartment," she said, thinking how odd it would be to leave her family home.

Living with them for twenty-four years was longer than she planned. After her parents learned of her pregnancy, they encouraged and helped her finish college while watching their grandson.

Because of their generosity, she had her bachelor's degree in elementary education. Leaving Trenton with her mother every day while she attended school, eased her mind that her son was looked after and so very loved.

Now, the time had come to grow up and face her responsibilities with a new husband.

Sipping the last of her bubbly, she thought back to that one night, when minus her panties, she let down her guard.

The superstition of dancing naked around the Cupid statue in the town square said the next person you met should be your true love. The consequences of her jaunt around that piece of rock appeared nine months later with the delivery of her beautiful baby boy.

Shame, his father didn't have the courage to listen to her when she tried to tell him the results of their one night together where even a condom didn't stop her from getting pregnant. Instead, he'd been too busy going off to graduate school than to learn they were expecting.

One day when Trenton was old enough, they would have a long talk about his father. It would be hard to keep the bitterness from her voice and the anger from her words. His father followed his dreams while she had their child.

"If you decide against this wedding, you're welcome to escape to the family cabin on the banks of the Leon River right outside Bride, Texas. That crazy little town started by the jilted bride."

"A jilted bride started that hole in the wall?"

"Yes, she was stood up by her fiancé and she created a life for herself right there. A beautiful story to remind brides that sometimes there is something better coming along," Ally said, smiling. "It's one of the reasons I like it there."

"Thank you, but I won't need a place. I'm getting married in twenty-four hours."

"Well, here's the key to the cabin," Ally said, dangling the metal like a temptation. "I'll carry it in my bouquet, just in case."

Laney giggled. "Thanks, but next week, I'll be moving into Roger's apartment as his wife and he as Trenton's father."

Ally took a deep sigh and released it. "You realize you have the worst luck with guys. What makes you think marriage will be any better?"

"Yes, I agree I'm unlucky when it comes to men," she said, her eyes blinking with unshed tears.

This was her second endeavor at standing before a preacher and saying vows. Not long after the birth of Trenton, she met Jim who asked her to marry him, only six weeks before the ceremony, he walked away. Disappeared without a call, without a trace.

An unplanned pregnancy, a broken engagement, and now the night before her big day, she had jitters. Nothing more than nerves.

Ally shook her head. "Don't know why, I always thought you would wed Chase. Ever since my brother picked you up that night we dared you to dance in the buff around Cupid, I pictured the two of you together."

"Sometimes even Cupid gets it wrong," she said, knowing she thought she would wed him as well.

✒

Laney stood in the vestibule of the church, in her white satin dress and veil waiting for the wedding march to begin. Doubts assailed her like hail in a Texas thunderstorm. Just like Ally had the night before, she questioned if she should marry Roger.

A gorgeous, rock-solid man who had a great job, supported her, treated her special, kissed well...*but not as earth moving like the man who broke your heart,* her conscious reminded her.

Reaching up, she touched the gold heart necklace, still wondering who had sent her the jewelry. Not long after she did the Cupid dance, it arrived in an unmarked box. No return address, no name, nothing. Now, she considered it her lucky charm.

"Are you certain?" her father asked. "It's not too late to back out."

"Let's go, Daddy," she said, refusing to let her apprehension overcome her. "He's a good man."

"Yes, he is," her father replied. "Is he the right man for my daughter?"

"Come on, Dad. They're waiting," she said, plastering a smile on her face, not answering. That would be a long discussion. One they didn't have time for.

"Okay, let's go," he said and patted her on the hand.

Walking down the aisle, she barely glanced at the people who were seated. Her eyes were on the man she was about to commit her life to, hoping she was making the right choice.

As she neared Roger, she noticed he appeared anxious. Sweat

121

beaded on his forehead. Of course, he was nervous. They were making a lifetime commitment today. A major life event.

Smiling, she tried to reassure him as she approached the altar.

"Who gives this woman away?"

"Her mother and I," her father said, handing her off to Roger. Placing her hand in his, she gave a quick, reassuring squeeze.

The pastor looked out at the people gathered for the ceremony. "Should there be anyone who has cause why this couple should not be united in holy matrimony, please say so now."

The door of the church slammed open and the sound of high-heels running down the aisle had her frowning as she watched Roger's eyes widened, his mouth dropped open, and she knew. Like a bolt of lightning, she just knew...

The color faded from her fiancé's face as he gasped, and her stomach tightened. Taking a deep breath, she fortified herself for the bad news. Unlucky again.

"Excuse me, but this man is married," a shrill voice sounded as their friends and family mumbled to each other.

A short woman with bottled-blonde hair and a set of decorated designer boobs displayed down to the top of her nipples, stood waving a piece of paper, a hefty rock on her left hand. "This is a copy of the marriage license. I have a ring on my finger and our wedding photo."

Reaching for her beacon of hope, Laney's fingers flew to the golden heart necklace around her throat.

Relief seemed to flood Laney and the look of horror on Roger's face made her burst out laughing. From the distress etched on his face, she grasped the woman's claim was true. Anger flooded her body like a Texas downpour racing through the streets. The man who supposedly loved her let her make a complete fool of herself.

"You low-life jerk," she said low enough for only his ears. "You're married. When were you going to tell me?"

"No, no," he cried as she walked back down the petal covered carpet, her satin skirt swishing, determination in every step to elude this fiasco.

"The marriage is not real. It happened in Vegas," Roger howled. "Stop, Laney, stop."

"Oh, yes, it did," the woman said. "We met, spent the night together, and woke up the next morning in wedded bliss. After I went to get coffee, you left before we talked about where we're going to live."

"That was fake," he exclaimed.

"Oh no, baby. This sealed document is as real as it gets. You belong to me."

Nearing the heavily made-up woman, Laney sensed her parents surrounding her, her precious son in her mother's arms. The touch of her father's hand at her elbow, guiding her around the circus she could see unfolding there in the church, was comforting.

Roger begged his new wife to stop as she shoved the paper that shackled him to the platinum bombshell in his face. "Honey, I'm so glad I showed up. Bigamy is against the law."

"Right now, jail would be better than the hell I'm living."

The vulgar woman laughed. "That's not what you said in bed the other night."

Hurrying past the unfolding chaos, a loud scuffling noise came from behind. Looking over her shoulder to see Roger sprawled in the aisle, a satisfied look of retaliation spread on her grandmother's face.

Granny could be deadly with her cane, buying Laney time to escape the auditorium. Smiling at the woman she loved, she gave her a thumbs up.

Laney hurried out the chapel. Funny, she wasn't crying. She wasn't even sad. Actually, she felt at peace. As they reached the vestibule, she turned to her mother and took her son from her arms.

"What are you doing?" her mother asked, emerald eyes filled with tears.

"I'm leaving town for a little while," she said, knowing instinctively this was what she should do. Hide out from the drama swirling around her and Roger. Getting away was the only reason she would have any serenity. Moving as swift as her taffeta skirt would allow, she made her way past the stunned wedding planner.

"Let me keep Trenton," her mother said, running after her.

"Thank you, Mom, but I need my son. Give me a chance to get away, and I promise, I'll call you later. At the moment, I must leave."

The impulse to race as fast as she could from the scene of her latest disaster sped through her like the adrenaline of running. The fight or flight urge was all flight. The flaxen-haired sex kitten could have Roger.

In a fog, she entered the bride's room, picked up the overnight bag. Trenton would need more clothes in a few days or a washing machine would work, but she didn't care. Thank goodness, her suitcase was already in the trunk of her car.

Soon as she could grab the rest of her stuff, she would run out the building, though she had no plan where she would go.

Following behind her into the suite, her mother's face was streaked with tears. A distressed frown crinkled her father's forehead as he tried to comfort her mother while he scrutinized his daughter.

"Mom, I'm all right. Let me slip away so Roger can't reach me. The wedding was ruined by his lovely new wife and I hope they're very unhappy together."

"Your mother stopped me from punching him," her father said. "I wanted to deck him."

"Thank you," she said, her heart aching for the hurt her parents were feeling as she reached over and kissed them each on the cheek. Just then, she heard Roger's voice yelling for her at the top of his lungs.

"Mom, Dad, I'm sorry, I've got to get out of here. Trust me, I'm okay, but I don't want to speak to him."

Reaching into his pocket, her father pulled out a wad of cash. "In case you need something. Don't forget to call. We'll be waiting to hear from you."

"As soon as we arrive," she said and squeezed her mother's arm.

"Be careful," her mother said and her father wrapped her in his arms.

Picking up her bags, Laney rushed down the hall to the chapel exit, her wedding dress swishing. If only she had time to change clothes. At the door, she saw Ally leaning against the frame, twirling a key.

"Told you so," she said and handed her the shining metal.

"I don't..." The cabin was the perfect place. A small little house tucked on the river, away from town, away from everyone until the melodramatics died down. The kind of place to disappear for a while. Soak up the sun and rest.

"The weather is supposed to become nasty later today, so be watchful. Call me if you have any trouble," Ally said. "Even if you want a little company."

Laney gave her an awkward hug. "This is why I love you. Trenton and I will enjoy the solitude and the quiet."

When the dust settled, she would tell Ally how right she was about her luck with men, but right now, she had to leave or face Roger.

"Now, go. Somehow a reporter showed up and is wanting to do a story on the Unlucky Bride. An interview you don't want to give."

A sarcastic laugh bubbled up from within her. "Why do I have the worst luck when it comes to men?" A glance at her son and her heart swelled with love. "Except that one time I got you, buddy."

"Go," Ally commanded. "And be careful of the—"

Suddenly a flash bulb went off in her face. Ducking her son's head, she ran to her car - all decorated with streamers announcing they were man and wife.

A curse slipped from her lips.

"No, Mommy, bad word," Trenton told her.

"You're right, son. Mommy won't say it again," she promised.

"Where's Roger?" he asked.

"Gone for good," she said and buckled him in his seat.

Starting the car, she drove out of the parking lot, prophylactics flying from her grill, tin cans bouncing behind her, streamers proclaiming just married. More like, publicly dumped.

Thunder rumbled, the house shuddering as Chase Hamilton stared out the window at the rain streaming from the sky. Why in the hell had he come here to this little cabin in the middle of godforsaken nowhere?

Growing up in Cupid, Texas, where people danced naked around a boy in a diaper sculpture to find their true love, he was shocked to learn how a jilted woman started this beautiful community. His parents' weekend getaway sat about a hundred feet from the Leon River, right outside Bride, Texas - where jilted women sought answers to their love life.

What about cheated on men? Where did they go?

To a home along the Leon River to heal. Two broken ribs, a black eye, and a bruised heart. In an irresponsible act of rage, he threw the first punch, creating a scene and barely escaping arrest. All because Cissy, who he enjoyed dating, didn't believe in monogamy. Now, he asked himself, had she been worth all the pain and anger.

Hell, no.

Limping away from the window, he sank back onto the couch, placing the ice pack on his bruised body. Staring at the blank screen of the television, he pondered his life, taking stock of where to go from here.

"Fighting is for losers," he said out loud, his brain agreeing with him. His heart saying *come on, you'd punch the jerk again.*

You don't hit women, children, or animals and the man had done two out of three in front of Chase causing him to lose his meager self-control.

Sadly, Cissy's dramatics outweighed the positives and left him reeling. In the end, she'd chosen the muscled brute over Chase, regardless that the wrestler kicked her dog and slapped her beautiful face.

That kind of crazy, he didn't need - though until then, she seemed so perfect.

Headlights flashed through the darkened room and slowly he rose to his feet. Who could be driving out here in this awful weather? No one knew he had escaped here to lick his wounds and mend in private.

A small Honda splashed on the dirt drive leading to the house. What were they doing coming out here now?

The car stopped and a woman opened the car door and stepped out. Her head bent to avoid the slashing rain drops as she reached inside the backseat of the car. As the woman turned and faced him, his chest tightened, his stomach churned, and he couldn't believe his eyes.

Laney Baxter in a long, lace wedding dress dashed through the puddles running toward the cabin, a little boy in her arms. The memory of their one night together slammed into his gut, wrenching his very soul and he groaned. Not what his recovery needed.

Stepping under the awning, she set the child down and he

heard the key in the lock. Chase yanked the door open and she jumped back, her eyes wide with fright.

"Chase," she said in shock, her emerald eyes widening. How he loved gazing into her eyes, feeling like he'd come home.

Shaking his head, he confirmed his eyes weren't betraying him, she was indeed wearing a wedding gown.

"Where's the groom?"

"Left him at church," she said, emptying water out of her shoes.

"What the hell are you doing here? Where did you get a key?"

"Ally told me I could use the cabin for a while."

"Well, she's wrong. You've got to leave."

Laney reached up and ran her hand through her wet hair and glanced down at her son who stared up at her in confusion. "Momma?"

"Ally didn't tell me you would be here. I'm sorry," she said. "I thought I would be alone."

"She doesn't know I'm here. No one knows and I want to keep it that way."

"Little late for that," she said. "When I return, she's going to want to know why."

The little boy tugged on the tulle of her gown and Chase wondered what happened that she came here and not on her fabulous honeymoon.

"Momma," he said a little louder.

How could a man or a woman hit a child or an animal? Yes, he'd been wrong to stoop to the man's level, and yes, he was paying the price for his rage. When his fist connected with the tough wrestler's cheek, the explosion of flesh and bone felt good, until his retaliation shot landed in Chase's ribs.

Never one to wrestle and throw a punch quickly, he had been no match against the professional.

Glancing down at the child, the vision of a screaming toddler invading his personal space made his decision. They had to leave.

"Tell her you couldn't reach the house. Tell her anything. But you can't stay here."

"You're going to send us back out into the storm," she said, her eyes narrowing.

The two of them shared one magical night of being together, and right now, his heart was dealing with his latest love disaster leaving him vulnerable. Too vulnerable to the charms of Laney. Even in her wet, muddied, now ruined, wedding dress, her mahogany hair falling around her shoulders, she looked stunning.

Whatever happened, the man had been a fool to let her go, and Chase couldn't be around her. Not now, not even with a downpour raging outside. She was hurricane force winds of danger compared to cold front Cissy.

"Momma, I need to go potty," the little boy said impatiently. "Now."

"Can my son at least use your restroom before we go back out into the storm?"

A twinge of guilt gripped him and his logical side reminded him of the dangers.

"Of course," he said. He wasn't a complete monster. Just a man confused and hurt and trying to recover.

Taking the boy by the hand, she led him into the living area and straight to the bathroom. In fewer than five minutes, they returned.

"Come on, son, let's go."

"We're not staying?"

"No, we're not," she said defiantly and walked out the door without saying goodbye. "Men are such dicks."

Peering out at the pouring rain, he watched from the door as she loaded the little boy into the child seat in the back of the car. Regret ate at his insides, he should stop her. The thought of a kid running through the house, making noise and the constant presence of Laney kept his lips shut.

Climbing into the car, she started the vehicle and backed away.

Chase closed the door, the silence eating at him. He should have let her stay. Frustrated, but thinking he'd been heartless, he yanked open the door to stop her. Running into the rain after her, to keep her from going, all he saw were tail lights going down the long drive.

One minute, he was trying to save someone and getting injured in the process, and the next, he was sending a woman and child out in a storm. Maybe she was right. Maybe he was just as much of a dick as Cissy's new love.

Available At All Retailers!

Secrets, Lies and Online Dating

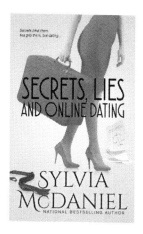

One event changes the lives of three women.

A lie changes Marianne Larson's perfect world leading her on a journey of self discovery. Brenda Jones, her mother, objects to being left behind and sets off on her own adventure. Katie Larson starts college and discovers that growing up is not as easy as she originally thought.

Can three generations recreate their lives and learn that their bond is stronger than secrets, lies, and on-line dating?

Available at Amazon!

Contemporary Romance
Return to Cupid, Texas
Cupid Stupid
Cupid Scores
Cupid's Dance
Cupid Help Me!
Cupid Cures
Cupid's Heart
Cupid Santa
Cupid Second Chance
Return to Cupid Box Set Books 1-3

Contemporary Romance
My Sister's Boyfriend
The Wanted Bride
The Reluctant Santa
The Relationship Coach
Secrets, Lies, & Online Dating

Bride, Texas Multi-Author Series
The Unlucky Bride

The Langley Legacy
Collin's Challenge

Short Sexy Reads
Racy Reunions Series
Paying For the Past
Her Christmas Lie
Cupid's Revenge
Science/Fiction Paranormal
The Magic Mirror Series
Touch of Decadence

Touch of Deceit

Also By Sylvia McDaniel

Western Historicals
A Hero's Heart
Ace's Bride
Second Chance Cowboy
Ethan

American Brides
Katie: Bride of Virginia

The Burnett Brides Series
The Rancher Takes A Bride
The Outlaw Takes A Bride
The Marshal Takes A Bride
The Christmas Bride
Boxed Set

Lipstick and Lead Series
Desperate
Deadly
Dangerous
Daring
Determined
Deceived

Scandalous Suffragettes of the West
Abigail
Bella
Callie – Coming Soon
Faith
Mistletoe Scandal

Southern Historical Romance
A Scarlet Bride

The Cuvier Women
Wronged
Betrayed
Beguiled
Boxed Set

Want to learn about my new releases before anyone else? Sign up for my New Book Alert and receive a free book.

USA Today Best-selling author, Sylvia McDaniel is an award-winning author of over forty western historical romance and contemporary romance novels. Known for her sweet, funny, family-oriented romances, Sylvia is the author of The Burnett Brides a historical western series, The Cuvier Widows, a Louisiana historical series, Lipstick and Lead, a western historical series and several short contemporary romances.

Former President of the Dallas Area Romance Authors, a member of the Romance Writers of America®, and a member of Novelists Inc, her novel, A Hero's Heart was a 1996 Golden Heart Finalist. Several other books have placed or won in the San Antonio Romance Authors Contest, LERA Contest, and she was a Golden Network Finalist.

Married for over twenty years to her best friend, they have two dachshunds and a good-looking, grown son who thinks there's no place like home. She loves gardening, hiking, shopping, knitting and football (Cowboys and Bronco's fan).

www.SylviaMcDaniel.com
The End

49497665R00082

Made in the USA
San Bernardino, CA
22 August 2019